Alley Waif

A Story of Second Chances

FRANK MARSEGLIA

MILES TO GO PUBLISHING • ASHLAND, OREGON

Alley Waif: A Story of Second Chances
by Frank Marseglia
© 2018 Frank Marseglia
Published by Miles To Go Press
Framarpublishing@gmail.com

Editor: Kit Crumb
Author photos: Diana O'Farrell
Book & Cover Design: BookSavvyStudio.com

ISBN: 978-1-7327763-0-2
First Edition
Printed in the United States of America

CONTENTS

PROLOGUE

SHE KNEW SHE HAD TO FIND A PLACE out of the wind, one where she could keep reasonably warm and hopefully dry. This camp had become too crowded and the leers of the homeless men too frequent. She tried keeping to herself, to make herself smaller, but the hunger in their eyes was apparent and growing. Her large heavy coat was too much of a prize for someone who wore worn and tattered clothing. And once they got up the nerve to take it, what else would they want. She had to protect herself one night. One of the men tried to take her coat and she swiped at his fingers with her knife. She decided to leave the tenuous comfort of homeless camp in the morning and find another temporary home.

She'd been searching the streets for a place to stay, her new home, for the past two days. The places she found were too out in the open or they too were over crowded. She slept in the doorway of an abandoned store the night before. Wind and constant noise of cars and pedestrians woke her every few minutes to find herself shivering. Even the heavy mover's quilt she wrapped around her body didn't stop her didn't provide enough warmth to let her go back to sleep.

While searching, she studied the people who scurried or rambled by. Once in a while she would see a young woman with black hair and blue eyes. When she tried to talk to them, but they would get angry and bark at her or look away in disgust and rush off. Some would reach into their pockets for change and afraid they might contract whatever she had, drop it on the ground.

As dusk settled, her stomach grumbled with the reality she hadn't eaten all day. She walked by a Chinese restaurant with an alley on the side. It wasn't very long, but the end seemed to be lit by two lights. She stood still watching for any movement before she entered. Knowing the restaurant would have a back door with garbage cans, she tip-toed the length carefully. It wasn't wide by any means, maybe just enough to back a large truck down for backdoor deliveries and to pick up the refuse of three dumpsters at the end. Stopping half-way down, she realized it had two legs at the end of it, reminding her of a 'T'. The back door of the Chinese restaurant was on one leg and on the other, the back door of a pizza parlor. She smiled, *I could have Italian one night and Chinese another.* Both were lit by a light above the kitchen doors.

Standing at the end, she peeked around the corner of the left leg. There stood three garbage cans. Careful not make any noise, she walk up to them and opened one of the lids. She could hear the sound of dishes clinking together, angry voices in Chinese yelling out orders, pots banging on hard surfaces and the smell of cooking coming out through the roar of an exhaust fan. She looked at the door hoping it wouldn't open. Satisfied, her hand searched the warm remnants of the latest lunch session. It didn't take long to find enough food to satisfy her hungry stomach. Closing the lid silently, she turned to inspect the rest of the alley.

A loud bump emitted from the restaurant door like something hitting it. She jumped and in a panic ran around the corner of the alley. Ducking down, she peeked around the edge of the building and watched a man in a white T-shirt enter the alley. His shadow loomed well ahead of his body from the kitchen light as he struggled to carry a large plastic container. Once he stood in front of the three garbage cans he took off the lid of the middle one and emptied the smaller container into one of the cans she'd been rummaging through. The woman held her breath, as if its vapor cloud would give away her position. The man straightened up and spun around looking to where the woman was crouched. Plumes of white billowed into the air as he yelled something to the people inside. Flapping his arms, he started to inspect the alley. The woman was about to edge back toward the street. Someone inside hollered. He yelled back to his co-workers and she heard loud laughter. The man picked up the can and returned to the kitchen slamming the door. She heard it bang closed and peeked around the corner and waited for five minutes.

Creeping out from the corner, she began to inspect the alley. There was a large, flattened box, the kind you'd ship a stove at the end of the alley next to a dumpster. She opened one of the dumpster lids and climbed in and started to feel around for something useful. Within a few minutes her hand latched onto a blue tarp. She yanked and yanked on it, but it wouldn't budge. Her face flushed realizing she was standing on part of it. *Stupid.* Moving to one side, she pulled hand over hand until it came free of its trappings. A smile formed. She held it up inspecting it. It had only one large hole on the end.

Dragging the tarp over to the large box, she laid it flat on top of it. It was large enough to cover three sides of the box. "Yes!" She said gleefully. If nothing else it might keep her dry if it rained. She pulled the box over to the corner, not far from the rear entrance of the pizza parlor and cleared out a space. Lifting one corner of the box until it stood up, she tucked the flaps into one another so it wouldn't fall flat again. She kneeled in front, unwrapped the mover's blanket from inside her coat and laid it on the bottom of the box. She crawled into it and sat looking out of her new home smiling.

◆ ◆ ◆

A man stared straight out into a vast emptiness, the leafless trees and people who walked by where invisible to him. In his mind he was younger barking out orders to still younger men and women eager to obey his every command. Today, short cropped hair tickled his head as it waved in the late October wind. The creases on his forehead and his downturned mouth told all passersby that he did not want to be disturbed. His hand reached for the cane beside him as he let out a sigh. Bending over in the middle the man rose from his seat in the park and slowly walked home to his warm apartment and loving wife.

◆ ◆ ◆

She stood in front of the fireplace, arms folded across her chest gazing sadly at the photographs of her daughter and grandchild. They stared in lonely silence back at her with rueful smiles. She longed for their visits and the continuous noise that would fill the apartment. Next to them was a picture of a young woman in a silver-blue dress with her hand wrapped around the arm of a man in a Marine Corps dress blue uniform. The look on their faces showed that was the happiest day of their lives. Sunlight glinted off their shiny new gold wedding bans.

The cuckoo clock on the wall chimed one. The woman looked to the door hearing a metallic sound. Her smile returned.

CHAPTER ONE

I HEARD THE TWO-PITCHED SCREECH, long and loud. Its counter-screech was just as imposing only in a different pitch seeming older and stronger. Ice cold gale-force wind pushed against my body causing me to stagger occasionally. It felt like I was pulling a weighted sled up the street, step by painful step. In seconds it stopped and the sudden calm overwhelmed me. The screeching continued with hissing and spitting echoed by the tinkling of glass and clanging of empty cans. I turned my head and stopped. The tip of my nose felt numb and the tops of my ears burned with icy stiffness. With my cane in my left hand, my right pulled the collar of my overcoat tight beneath my chin catching the tears that trickled down my cheeks leaving frozen straight lines. The wind picked up again with renewed strength and my short gray hair fluttered as my trousers whipped in the late November wind.

People passed me with heads bowed rushing home, none looked up to see why an old man would stand in the middle of the sidewalk and take such punishment. Some clutched bags tightly to their chests or firmly under an arm. Those with nothing to carry stuck their hands deep into their pockets. With up-turned collars and hunched shoulders, those coming toward me were glad to have the wind at their back; the rest just had to deal with the onslaught.

Following the sound, I stepped into the alley leaving the turbulence of the street behind. The air turned calm and still except for the two cats angrily locked in battle shrieking and spitting at each other. They were at the end of a well-lit intersection. Claws scratching and fangs gnawing into their opponent's fur and flesh, they tumbled scattering bottles and cans. After seconds of furious combat they broke apart hissing with mouths wide open and bared teeth. One slinked back and crouched ready to defend itself; the larger of the two cats sat licking its paw with tail swishing on the asphalt, a chicken leg lay a few inches away, the prize for the victor. It was only a small scrap with a bit meat, some slimy skin and gristle, but to them it might be a whole meal and an end to the search for food on this frigid night.

The larger cat stopped licking its paw, turned to its opponent and hissed. It knew it had won and there would be no more fighting. It stood up slowly keeping an eye on its opponent and picked up its reward in its jaws. With the leg in its mouth, it padded away triumphantly, tail straight up in the air, as if saying. "Kiss my ass." It didn't look back.

The smaller cat watched its rival prance away. Its mouth opened in a silent protest. It jumped onto a box, then bounded onto a dumpster and finally leaped to a fire-escape. It settled down on the iron grating with its head protruding through the railing gazing intently to the left with paws grasping the edge. Tail swaying, it watched something of extreme interest.

That's when I heard a soft, melodic female voice, "Kitty, kitty." Then another chicken leg arced through the air landing almost in the same spot as the other leg.

The cat vaulted from the fire-escape in a single bound and snatched up the leg. Ignoring me, it sped out of the alley and down the street with its long thin tail trailing.

Curious, I inched my way into the alley. Who was the cat's benefactor? I smiled, as I entered thinking, 'Curiosity killed the cat.' Metallic sounds of a garbage can lids echoed off the brick walls. I decided whomever it was would not hurt me, so I continued.

Illuminated by a light above a door, a woman rummaged through a garbage can as steam from the warm refuse escaped mixing with the steady puffs of her breath forming a white haze. She wore a dark, heavy coat that hung down past her knees. A navy knit hat, the kind sailors wore while on watch on cold winter's nights, covered her head and pulled down over her ears with tufts of dark hair sticking out in every direction. Above her and above the door a sign read, "Mr. Lim's Chinese Restaurant."

Moving further into the depths of the alley, the stench of garbage and urine caused me to want to gag. Still, I inched forward.

The woman, so engrossed in her task didn't hear me approach. I kept my distance. She reached down into the depths of the middle of three garbage cans moving her hand from side to side looking for bits of food. The back of her coat exhibited stains of accumulated dirt and grime. Silently, I watched her. I don't know why I felt nervous, but my heart pounded.

Finding a large piece of chicken, she stood straight up, brushed it off and put it to her nose. She examined it again and nibbled the end. After looking at it once more, she stuffed the whole piece into her mouth. I felt pity for this old woman who had to scrounge around restaurant garbage to stay alive. She had no bags at her side as most other wretched souls who live on the street. No cart, no means to carry the small treasures that make life just a little easier.

The wind gusted hard into the alley swirling paper in all directions. Small lighter pieces flew in a whirlwind trying to find a means of escape into the night sky. I scanned the rest of the alley and noticed a large cardboard box. Big enough to ship a stove in, the box lay in another lit corner covered by a blue tarp ten feet from the back door of a pizza parlor. I imagined she would probably look in their garbage cans on another night. The box was empty except for a blanket and some odds and ends. I realized this alley and that cardboard box was her home and it held all she owned.

I stepped forward just an inch or two. She must have heard the crunch of broken glass because she suddenly spun around. Clutching her coat with her right hand, her left slid into a pocket. Socks worn on her hands with the toes cut out displayed slimy finger tips from digging in the garbage. She stared at me with fear, embarrassment and then anger. She stepped back a few steps falling into the light showing the grime on her face and wind-blown cracked lips. To my horror, I was looking at a young girl, no more than thirteen or fourteen years of age.

I gasped. How could such a young thing be cast out into the streets to search for food in garbage cans especially at a time when families are making arrangements for holiday gatherings? A thousand more questions invaded my mind, all of which I had no answers, at least ones that would make sense or give a viable reason.

"Hello," I said with a cracked voice. I couldn't think of anything else to say.

She stood staring at me with unwavering eyes and in the intensity of their hate, I felt threatened. It would have been funny if someone else had told me of this encounter. I realized that the unease I was experiencing was the fact that it was so unexpected.

"Uh," I thought fast. "I'm sorry, I didn't..."

She glared at me not saying a word, not moving a muscle. Her eyes grew fiercer. I have seen these eyes many times before, wary and attuned to the nuisances of an enemy's movement. She had the look of a predator, who at any second would strike out with the sole purpose of harming me. Only she wasn't a predator, she was a child. Sure, I remember in my youth fighting along-side and against children like her, but those were different times and different places, certainly not the United States of America. I thought back to my child at that age. Her eyes held nothing but love, trust and happiness. I would never have cast her out to search for food, no matter what the justification.

My heart stopped pounding and settled down to its normal rhythm. I slipped off a glove, reached into my pocket and pulled out a twenty dollar bill. I held it out.

She still did not move and continued to stare at me in distrust. I moved a step forward.

Her hand came out of her pocket with such speed I only saw a blur. Her fingers grasped a shiny metal object. Her thumb pressed a button and 'swith' a four inch blade appeared, finely sharpened and glinting in the light, she stood her ground. She held her arm slightly up toward me with the knife in her hand steady and ready for anything.

I felt tongue-tied, what do you say to a person you want to help, but only wants to be left alone? So I extended my hand a little further, hoping to show her I meant no harm. She made no move toward me nor away, but the look in her eyes turned to rage. Did I offend her? I should have known she wouldn't reach for the money. Did I over-step my bounds by offering it? Making a hasty retreat would be the best plan of action, I thought. I turned to go and spied a brick on the ground.

I motioned to it holding my hands out, a sign of non-aggression. "I'll just place this under the brick. If you want it you can take when I'm gone." She made no indication either way.

I bent over while keeping an eye on this unfortunate stray. I tucked the twenty under the brick, straightened up and started to walk away. I stopped and turned around. She stood still. Watching. I reached into my coat pocket and pulled out a tube of ChapStick and tossed it to her. She caught it adeptly with her right hand. I nodded to the young woman and exited not looking back and enraging her even more. I felt unsettled. I wanted to do more, but what could I do?

Once again on the street I turned toward the pub I frequented and was immediately buffeted by the wind. I decided I would give this some more thought. Once inside the door, the heat of the place struck me as overwhelming. The laughter and merriment was quite a difference to the scene in the alley. I sidled up to the bar and took a seat.

◆ ◆ ◆

Angry with herself, the young woman realized she had been so engrossed in finding food that she'd let her guard down and in doing that she became vulnerable. "That was close, too close," she murmured.

The man scared her, she couldn't stop shaking. Walking over to the brick, she picked up the twenty dollar bill then looked down at the entrance of the alley to make sure he didn't return. Holding the money up to the light, she stuffed the bill into her pants pocket smiling and then scratched her head. She applied the Chap Stick to her lips, "cherry," and stuffed the tube into her coat pocket. She snatched a look at the entrance one more time, turned and walked back to the far corner of the alley and her box.

The wind roared into the alley. Paper blew in circles rustling and skittering across the asphalt. Cans tumbled around making an empty metallic sound only to be answered by the high pitch of wine bottles rolling. The young woman shivered violently looking up at walls of the three ancient apartment buildings. Windows glowed with yellow warmth, as inhabitants returned home for the evening. Gray clouds blanketed the sky covering the few stars seen at night in a city. She decided her box would be warmer than the air outside and having eaten, she crawled into her temporary home. She found her water bottle and took a small drink, then poured water on a rag and scrubbed her face and hands. She closed the flaps blocking the light and pulled a frayed movers quilt over her body and closed her eyes.

The man who left her the money kept seeping into her mind, she had seen him several times before in the park. It was a good idea to know who belonged in the neighborhood and who didn't. He usually sat by himself feeding squirrels and seldom had any contact with other people. Often he would sit staring out into space with sad vacant eyes and a down-turned mouth. She even walked by him several times while he fed the squirrels. He never noticed her, like she was a ghost or a reflection in a window. She knew he was tallish and had a pencil thin mustache and on one cheek he has a straight white line from ear to mouth. Even though, he wore a heavy overcoat she could tell he had a strong frame. He sat with an erect posture and his hair cut a lot shorter than most men, she imagined him a retired servicemen. He looked like the grandfather she always wished she had. Someone she could ask for advice or give her direction, someone who would protect her from the evils of the world, but then she knew if anyone was going to protect her it would be her alone.

Still, it would be a good idea to keep her wits about her. Something about him made her think he wasn't completely harmless, despite the cane and almost unnoticeable limp. It wasn't the way he said hello, in that he was direct. She could tell she surprised him. No, it was his eyes, she thought. They seemed wary and scanning his environment for danger, just like her. After the initial shock of seeing her, his eyes were steady like his extended hand and they looked directly into her eyes, not straying. They seemed to take in everything in a single gaze. This old man wasn't a fool, nor, she was sure someone to be trifled with. A girl grew up fast on the street if she wanted to survive. Still, he left her some money and for that she was grateful. Some men offered her money, but they wanted something for it. Others offered, but when she would glare at them they would put it back in their pockets and walked away.

After a few minutes the warmth within the box and a hard day's scrounging began to take its toll on her and she drifted off into a dream world. It was a world where she was united with her sister who had been torn from her ten years ago. In this dream she slept in a warm safe place where she didn't have to watch every move she made and she could be fourteen again. She wanted a life where she had plenty to eat and was clean. Being clean for her took precedence over food. She could live on scraps, as she had been for six months. But she hated the feeling of being dirty and the sour smell of her body and the greasiness of unwashed hair. The look people gave her, when she entered a store, embarrassed her. She hated how their noses would crinkle and heads would turn aside as they stepped away from her. Even though, she tried to shower when she could at a shelter and wash in restrooms where the manager would let her, it wasn't enough. She wanted to be clean, really clean, squeaky-clean.

From the shadow of a doorway, a man watched the encounter between the young girl and the old man. He saw him slip something under a brick. A toothy grin spread across his face. He knew what transpired, Max wasn't a fool. He also knew that he would have to deal with a wild cat. The young girl already cut him once when he tried to take her coat a month ago, but he wanted the money. His eyes followed the old man down the street and enter a bar in the middle of the block. He waited a few seconds for a car to go by and stepped into the open. Immediately he felt the onslaught of the wind funneling through the brick canyon. He tucked in his chin, lifted the collar of his coat pinching it closed with his right hand and hustled across the street.

Wearing layers of shirts and two jackets under his long thin army coat and several pairs of pants gave Max's skinny frame an almost obese appearance. Scratching vigorously at some unwanted pests under his black knit hat, he stopped at the alley entrance shivering in the wind scanning it for the chatter and tell-tail smoke of restaurant workers taking a cigarette break. Satisfied his encounter would be private he walked huddled past the brick and up to the young girl's blue-tarped box. He scanned the alley again, then up at the lit windows. All was as he wanted it to be, quiet.

◆ ◆ ◆

The young woman had just dozed off when she felt the box shake. Instinctively, she slid her hand into the left pocket of her coat and grabbed the knife.

"Hey, wake-up little girl," an accented voice gave a harsh whisper and the box rattled again.

She cringed and swore to herself. 'Max!'

"Come on," his patience wearing thin. After all, he would rather be in his own hidie-hole trying to keep warm. "I know you're in there. I saw you go in," he lied. Max couldn't see where she went from across the street, but she didn't know that. He shook the box harder.

The young woman heard the crinkling of the tarp being pulled back. She opened the flaps, stuck her head out and stared at two grimy sneakers, one with a hole in the big toe. She looked up at the man disturbing her sleep. The back-light of the pizza parlor gave Max an ominous look. "What do you want Max? I've had a long day." She ducked back into the box again. "Leave me alone," said the angry young woman in a muffled voice.

"I want you Ad-de-son." Max kicked the box and ripped off the rest of the tarp, "I want that money the old man left you. Consider it rent." Max's big smile uncovered a gold tooth which seemed bright next to yellowed teeth. He appeared in worse shape than Addison, poor, home-less and dirty. Although, his filthiness seemed caked on, this demonstrated a lack of respect for himself. Hers was circumstance.

"Come on little girl, hand it over," Max demanded. Moving to the side of the box, he kicked it violently. The tarp ruffled in a sudden wind and flew to a corner.

Addison huffed and pressed the release button on her knife. The blade swished open. She pushed the flaps out and was immediately shrouded in the hash light from the pizza parlor. She looked to the right and saw Max waiting expectantly. Staring down at her, he shifted from foot to foot shivering.

"Come on, give it up," he said impatiently. Flapping his arms as his teeth chattered.

"Max go away," she whined. "He didn't leave me anything."

"Oh, yes he did," he said triumphantly, "I saw him put it under the brick."

Addison cringed. She knew Max wouldn't leave her alone until he got the money or she made him leave. She also knew that if she gave in to him, he would relish in his triumph and never leave her alone.

Max stood grinning. The whites of his eyes pale yellow in the reflected light in the pizza parlor's back door. He stuck out his hand expecting Addison to hand over the money. In his mind he had already bought a sandwich and some beer.

Addison crawled out of the warm box, knuckles scraping on the ground, but refusing to let go of the knife. Getting up on one knee, she started to stand.

"Whoa!" Max jumped back two feet extending a hand halting her. The smile disappeared, wariness taking over. "Don't get up any further," he commanded. "Let me see your hands." He looked at her suspiciously. Addison looked up at him and lifted one hand, empty. "Last month you cut me."

She smiled, stood up facing Max and raised her left hand, knife out twisting it towards his face. "Come closer and I'll stick and twist." She's had it with him and wanted to show him that messing with her had consequences.

Max stood straight up, he was taller, but he knew Addison was mad enough to carry out her threat. He backed away looking at the blade glimmer in the light.

Holding up both hands, "Whoa... whoa, no need for that kind of talk," he said trying another tactic, "Giirrl, why can't we be friends. You help me, I'll help you. With me nobody will bother you." He held out his hands, fingers splayed showing he meant no harm.

"You're the only one that bothers me Max." She flicked the knife threateningly. He jerked his hands back.

Max unconsciously rubbed the cut on his right forefinger where Addison sliced him before when he tried to take her coat. It hurt for days and started to fester, that wasn't something he wanted repeated. His friendly demeanor disappeared. "I'm a better friend than an enemy, a young girl, like you, needs friends."

"Just leave me alone," she demanded. Addison stood her ground. She kept her eyes on Max desperately trying to control the shaking in her hand. She didn't want him to know she too was scared and not just for losing the money.

Max wanted the money, but most of all, he wanted this confrontation to end with him the winner. If she won, he would lose credibility as a tough thug. He had to relieve her of that knife, then he could get the money. Then he would have bragging rights that he bested the young girl. Max started to make small jerking motions toward Addison waiting for an opening. Addison countered quickly with her knife. He had to strike, but not at the price of getting stabbed in this damned dirty alley. Addison had to be put in her place. Max inched his leg back a bit. His heart pounded and his breath jagged, puffed out in spurts of white cloud and he felt fear grip him, but he had to take her, he had to.

They stood glaring at each other. Clouds of vapor pushed out by escalated breathing formed a gray haze, neither wanted to be the first to start something that would end up badly, for both of them.

The door of Mr. Lim's Chinese Restaurant opened. A young man in a white T-shirt and a stained apron carried out a garbage can, he looked at the two. "What you do? Get out, both you." He turned around and yelled something inside in his language. The next minute three people in white jackets came rushing out brandishing cleavers and knives. They moved out of the doorway toward the two homeless people forming a united front of four angry faces.

Max turned to look at the three chefs and dishwasher and knew it was time to leave. "O.K., O.K." he said bowing over and over, "I going." He turned back to Addison with a scowl, "I'll deal with you later." He backed out of the alley smiling and bowing, "So solly, so solly," he said, holding his hands together, as in prayer, showing his contempt for the restaurant workers.

Addison watched him go. Slowly her breathing returned to normal. Anger and fear turned into despair. *Why can't people leave me alone?* She walked past the angry stares and demeaning comments of the restaurant workers with her head bowed. Once on the street, she traveled in the opposite direction as Max.

Two hours later, huddling in a darkened alcove across the street from the alley, Addison scanned the neighborhood. She watched people walk up and down the sidewalk, checked other entryways for buffs of white and listened for any noise out of the ordinary. Invisible except for the vapor of her breath, she decided it was safe and sprinted for the alley. The clapping of her feet on the ground echoed loudly. As she turned the corner to her box, a figure stepped out in front of her grappling her by the waist. Addison's reflexes were fast, but Max's were faster. He grabbed her left wrist twisting it enough to make Addison cringe.

Addison screamed, "Ow! You're hurting me," jerking and twisting to get away.

Max swiftly released her waist. She tried to spin around, but not before he seized her throat whirling her around bashing her against a wall. He took pleasure at the thud of her head slamming into brick and her stunned pained expression.

Searing pain shot through Addison's head as dizziness overwhelmed her. Her knees buckled, but Max held her up with dirty fingers digging into the sides of her neck. As she struggled, his fingers dug deeper. She tried to pry his fingers away, but his grip hardened. She felt her arteries throb and a sense of weariness prevailed and she let her hand fall becoming compliant.

Looking at the fright on her face, Max grinned. "Not so tough now, are you?" He said with a toothy smile and leaned forward keeping a tight strangle-hold and reached into Addison's coat pocket.

Pulling out the knife, "I'll take this," he said triumphantly sliding it into a pocket of his coat. He awkwardly searched her coat pockets, but found nothing but a tube of chap-stick, he threw that away.

"I want the money," he whispered in her ear. He squeezed her cheeks with his free hand forcing her mouth open. His fingers slowly drew her cheeks together and sliding to the ends of her mouth scraping her skin. His thumb felt wet warmth of her inner lower lip. She made a move to nip his finger, but his other hand gripped a little tighter to warn her from doing anything stupid. A smile formed, "Yeah," he said as an urge began to build up inside of him. He felt his penis trying to straighten itself. He moved it around with his fingers. It was throbbing wanting to explode, a feeling he had to often take care of himself. *Maybe not tonight, maybe tonight is my lucky night. I might just forget the money and have a little fun, get it wet.* He thought about it for a second. *No, what would be nice is to get and get paid for it.* He felt like a little boy whose mother held out a cookie jar for him to pick out a cookie.

She recognized the gleam in his eyes and the way he licked his lower lip and knew exactly what was going on in his mind. Fear rose inside her, she couldn't help it and it was ready to explode. Even worse, she knew, he recognized her fear and he was relishing in it. He won.

"Yeah," he murmured. He pinched her lips again and snickered. His thumb rubbed the inside her lower lip a little deeper wetting it in her saliva. His erection strained to be let loose. He leered at her and took his finger out of her mouth putting it in his, tasting the wetness, savoring it. "I may have a taste of something else," he murmured enjoying the fear in her eyes.

Addison's legs shivered. Her cheeks hurt from Max's fingernails. She tasted acidic grime of his thumb. Her mouth betrayed her as it grew moist with spit. She thought of biting his thumb, but Max had her head in tight pinching grip. Staring into his eyes, she realized his hunger was growing. Suddenly, panic replaced pain. Her fear magnified ten-fold and she frantically squirmed to get away. Max chuckled, he was actually enjoying tormenting her. Addison felt a deeper feeling of panic than she ever experienced and tried to scream, but nothing could escape her mouth. She tried to grab his hand, but he pulled her toward him and slammed her against the wall. It hurt and scared her, but not as much as the thought of Max raping her. She tried to claw his eyes, but he bashed her even harder against the wall. A wave of dizziness overpowered her. Tears rolled down her cheeks as the helplessness grew. She became compliant.

Max unbuttoned her coat, "I'm gettin it... one way or nuther." His hand spread her coat open quickly and urgently. Smirking, he stared down at her. She averted her eyes. He unzipped her hoodie and spread that open. Then he tore the buttons from her shirt exposing bare skin.

She closed her eyes biting her lower lip tasting a bitter coppery liquid. Her breath was hard and fast.

His eyes lit up at the sight of her nipples, "I guess you like it rough," he said as his calloused hand cupped her breast, kneading it as a baker kneads dough, scraping the skin with sandpaper fingers. She tried to punch at his back, but he just tightened his grip on her throat. He pinched her breast with his fingers so the nipple stuck straight out and leaned over wrapping his lips around it. With his teeth, he bit down onto it. Addison groaned in pain. "You got small titties," he whispered into her ear.

She bit down harder on her lip, forcing herself to forget what Max was doing to her. Tears streamed down her cheeks. She whined and prayed for this to stop.

Max snorted and kissed her on the cheek. His tongue slid to the edge of her mouth and along her lip.

His stench made Addison's stomach convulse wanting to empty itself. She tried twisting her face one way or the other, but his mouth was right there wherever she twisted. Tears kept streaming from her eyes.

He drew away just a little, satisfied that he was in control. He moved his hand down to her belt and buckled it. She jerked and tried to claw his face to get away. Max drew her towards him then slammed her harder against the wall digging his nails deeper into her neck.

Addison wanted to scream for help, but the pressure on her throat kept anything but a gurgle from escaping.

Max unbuttoned and then unzipped her pants. He pawed his rough icy fingers onto the warm soft skin of her stomach and then slid his hand down until it snuck under her underwear. His excitement rose and he began to imagine taking her. Feeling silky hair, "You're kind of bushy." He felt like Christmas came early as he pulled a few strands of her hair. Addison winced and groaned. Max chortled.

"Back to business," he said and extracted his hand moving it to her pants pockets. He patted a pocket trying to feel if she hid money inside. Her hands tried to push his away, but he just squeezed her neck harder. "Co-operate, I'll get it anyway, it's just a matter of how much pain you want me to put on you," he chuckled as his fingers probed her crotch. *Maybe I should just forget the money for now and take her and then get the money when I'm through. The thought filled his brain. It's been too long.* He scanned the windows of the alley, nothing but yellow light through opaque shades. His breathing quickened as he started unbuttoning his coat.

There was no one here to save her. Addison knew it was all up to herself. Fighting down panic, she wrenched Max's wrist with both hands trying to pry his fingers from her throat. She twisted, pushed and yanked every way she could, "Le goo o mee." He was too strong and his nails dug deeper. She pushed up on his chin with one hand, but Max batted it away and punched her in the stomach. She gasped. She wanted to bend over to alleviate her agony, but he held her up.

"I'm gonna teach you." He leaned forward.

Addison reeled at the fetid smell of his breath. She struggled twisting her head away. Her stomach lurched into spasms, threatening an eruption. *Do it, do it* she thought, *chuck up all over him, maybe he'll let go and then I could run.*

Max snickered at her fear. His hand grabbed her face as he eased his wet tongue out at her. Starting from her below her jaw-line, he licked the side of her face. By the time he reached her temple his tongue was dry.

Addison jerked her knee up fast and hard, but Max turned slightly to the right. All she got was the side of his leg and a hard slap across the face, loud enough to echo in the quiet alley.

"Bitch." He held his hand up for a second blow.

Addison's fright succumbed to overwhelming rage. She spit at him.

Max screamed in a red fury. No bitch had ever spit into his face. He yanked her deeper into the alley. "Bitch, you're goin to learn a hard lesson," he yelled, but the bitch was strong and struggled every inch of the way.

She twisted hard and fast to the right loosening his grip. At the same time she stamped down grinding her heel on his exposed toe. Max shrieked. He released her throat temporarily bending over in pain. Addison screamed, "Help!" She kept screaming, hoping someone would come to her rescue.

Max's own anger took over and he pulled his fist back to strike her when he felt something grab his wrist twisting hard and fast, he heard a resounding snap. Within milliseconds, searing pain encompassed his whole being. Max shrieked again. It was all he could do.

Addison stood frozen, stunned for a second. She looked behind Max and saw a heavy gray overcoat, angry eyes over a scowl and a shock of gray hair. She knew it was the old man, quickly coming to her senses she scrambled out of the alley. Turning left at the entrance, she ran until her breath wouldn't allow her to run anymore, then she headed for the nearest blackened doorway.

Max fell on his back, legs splayed. Stunned when his head hit the frozen ground, he didn't know which hurt most the back of his head or his wrist. He looked up at his assailant. It was the old man. Through his tears, he saw rage in the old man's eyes and watched as the man's cane descended in a blur striking just above his forehead.

◆ ◆ ◆

Max stumbled out of the alley and hurried to the clinic a few blocks over. His body felt like one massive pain. He could only see out of one eye, blood from his forehead already coagulating and freezing his other eye closed. His wrist throbbed with as he cradled his hand in the other one. Every step or miss-step made it worse. His head had felt like someone was intermittently squeezing it, where he slammed it against the asphalt, after the old man jerked him backward and hit him on his forehead. Then there was a welt on his back where the old man hit him with his cane, as he was trying to escape, tripping him on his face breaking his nose.

As he entered the clinic, he vowed to get even with the old man and that little bitch. He vowed he would do it soon. He just needed to get his crew to help him. Max was sure once they saw him they'd fall over themselves to help him get his revenge.

The clinic was empty and quiet, except for the murmured laughter of the medical staff on this slow night. When Max walked up to the registration counter the two nurses on duty continued their conversation until he bellowed, "I need help." Then he began to knock on the counter with his good hand.

One gave him a disdained look. She began to take his information and then pointed to a seat for him to wait in until the doctor was finished with his patient. The other nurse came over to him, took his vital signs then checked probed and prodded his injuries.

Five minutes later the door to one of the examination rooms opened and an old lady hobbled out leaning heavily on her cane. As she walked by Max her cane hit him on the foot and he yelled out, "Watch it you old hag."

The doctor threw Max an angry glare and told him to enter the room.

Max explained to the doctor that he was jumped by four Caucasians, who kicked and punched him over and over.

"Don't worry," he said with a grin, "I got two of them."

He made jabbing motions with his good arm. The doctor raised his eyebrows disbelievingly. Max didn't notice, he was lost in a world of 'It could have happened.' When reality failed, the make believe world would suffice. If he kept telling it to himself enough, someday he might really think it was true.

"They probably be in later, after they wake up." His grin was convincing. "Yea! Fucked them up. They be sad for days."

The doctor on duty thoroughly checked Max out and noted only five injuries and none of them involved being kicked repeatedly. He packed Max's nose with soft gauze padding, sewed up his forehead and put on a cast on his wrist and gave him a sling for his arm. Before Max left, the doctor gave Max two pills; he said they would relieve the pain.

Max took the pills without water. When he received a prescription for more pills, Max's eyes lit up like he found the pot at the end of the rainbow. With a grin from ear to ear, he held the 'scrip' like it was made of solid gold and rushed to the pharmacy to get it filled.

CHAPTER TWO

MIRANDA CRAMER RECLINED in a corner of the sofa. The soft warmth of its fabric didn't generate its usual comfort. Tonight, its cushy confinement lent a feeling of sinking into an abyss of loneness. Richard should have been home an hour ago. He should have called if he was going to be this late, that is if he could, but the phone remained silent.

"If he could?" She mumbled. Those words, 'if he could', plagued her mind. Though the pub was only four blocks away, many things could happen in four blocks. "Stop!" She chided herself. *You're jumping to conclusions.* She sat biting her lower lip. *Maybe I should phone the bar.* No, she decided that would embarrass him. "Well that would serve him right for worrying me to death," she said to the empty apartment. *No, there must be an explanation.* But that didn't seem convincing or soothing either.

Staring at the copy of 'Scrubs', a nursing magazine in her lap, Miranda couldn't remember any of the articles she had read. The words blurred becoming black and white squiggles surrounded by unfocused images on the pages. Closing the periodical for the fifth time since Richard left, she tossed it on the coffee table. After the initial 'thwack' it hissed to the opposite side teetering between remaining on the table as a reminder of her unease and falling to the floor into oblivion she felt she was descending. She missed her career. She missed the excitement of the E.R. and training the young women to take her place. She longed for the reverence they gave her and how they would ask her advice from anything like the proper method of prepping a syringe to what to do if the man they loved was cheating on them. She felt she was in charge and now? She was just a retired old woman who would come by once a week and make a nuisance of herself.

Her eyes darted from the dangling magazine to the door, to the clock on the wall and back to the door. The room's quiet felt oppressive and lonely. There were no mutterings, no muffled curses, snickers or guffaws, no smiles and loving glances or pats on the hand, warm embraces or soft foot-pads in slippered feet on the carpet or many of the other ways Richard demonstrated he was here with her, if not at her side then close by.

No, the only sound was the slow methodical tick-tock of the coo-coo clock, an heirloom from her grandmother. As she looked at it, its sound amplified. Miranda watched the pendulum swing left with a 'tick' and right with a 'tock'. Her lips curled up into a sad smile as memories of 'Granny' flooded her mind. She watched the second hand move jerkily around the face, piling-up the seconds of Richard's lateness. At ten P.M. the little green door opened at the front and a red bird rushed out and coo-cooed ten times in a high pitch. Finished, it shuffled back inside and the door closed.

Below the clock stood a photograph of their daughter and grand-daughter smiling happily at her with hands raised in good-bye. Miranda's mind drifted back to that day and the sadness that ensued for weeks when her two most loved and favored people moved to Ashland, Oregon. That was six months ago and though Elizabeth calls every week to catch up, it's not the same as having lunch at Victor's or a day in the park's playground. Miranda realized that she had been holding that photo in her hand and didn't remember picking it up. She set it back on the mantle. It was a sad moment, one in which she felt she was saying good bye all over again.

Sporadic blips crashed against the living room window forcing memories to the back of her consciousness. Turning her head, Miranda gazed out into the night as the raindrops increased both in frequency and severity. Lights of the other apartment buildings checker boarded the darkness. Below she could see the tops of trees sway frantically in the glow of street lamps. And in the darkness of their living room window she saw the image of a sixty-two year old woman wishing her husband would walk through the front door.

Richard, if nothing, was precise and he was an hour late. Even though he would deny it, he was getting old and not the self-assured Marine he used to be. His career had ended two years ago, three months after hers, and he has been beside himself to come to terms with it. After all, he couldn't keep up with the younger men and women of today's Corps. There were too many scars, too much pain and he just didn't have to stamina.

She stared out of the window with her arms hugging herself lost in thought of the many times she worried about him when he was away on some foreign duty when a tiny metallic noise issued from the door and then a click. Miranda spun around, anxiety draining from her body. The handle twisted and the door opened. She caught her breath and everything that plagued her for the past hour fell into the same oblivion she felt moments ago. Richard was home. A smile crossed her face.

◆ ◆ ◆

The key turned smoothly in the lock ending with a soft click. Richard pushed opened the door and entered his apartment. Standing at the living room window, his wife of forty years breathed out a sigh of relief with a smile.

"You're home a little late Richard," Miranda said with a slight degree of reproof, she did not feel. Richard usually stayed out until nine P.M. when he visited the pub. The woman looked at the clock on the wall, it was ten thirty. She moved to the sofa and sat down waiting for his answer.

Richard slowly took off his gloves, then his rain-spotted coat, he shook it before hanging up on the coat rack. He removed his scarf hanging it next to his coat. He moved energetically to the sofa and sat beside the only woman he ever loved. She touched his cherry colored cheeks with the tips of her fingers. He felt the warmth, of not only her temperature but of her love.

"My God, your face is ice cold." She said shocked, "I'll make you some tea," and moved to get up, but Richard grasped her hand pulling her back down.

"Miranda," he said, "I've had the most amazing," his eyes lit up, "and yet frightening night, at least, since I retired. First, I found a woman, no a young girl rummaging through a garbage can….." He recounted the whole encounter of the young girl and then the hoodlum.

"On my way home from the pub, I heard a tussle in the alley. Afraid the young woman might be in grave peril, I entered. I found her struggling with a man who looked twice her size. It appeared he was trying to drag her deeper into the alley. I could only guess, to rape her. She put up a terrific fight, but I could see what the outcome would be." He showed his anger with these words, "He slapped her hard. The sound of it carried out to the street." He got off the sofa and animatedly pantomimed his actions. "My anger exploded and without any concern for my own safety, I rushed to her aid. I didn't yell or scream, although, in hind-sight, I probably should have. I guess my instincts were to take the thug by surprise. He drew back his fist to strike her again when I hooked my cane onto his wrist twisting hard and fast." He demonstrated with a swift twisting, jerking move.

Miranda started to rise from the sofa looking at him aghast, then she settled back down to let him finish the story.

"I heard his wrist snap," his eyes lit back up at the memory of the moment. "It sounded like a pretzel stick breaking, one of the fat ones. I yanked my cane back, with his limp wrist within the curved end yanking him onto the ground. Anger still surged through me and gave him a sharp blow to the forehead," his hand made a chopping motion, "sending him into a semi-unconscious state. I stood over him until he regained awareness. He lay on his back. A knife had fallen out of his pocket and lay next to him, I kicked it away. Blood seeped from below his hat forming a small steaming pool." Miranda winced at the image of that.

"I held my cane at his throat pressing slowly. His fear was evident by the look on his face. I told him if I ever saw him again, I would snap his neck as easily as his wrist. I asked him if he understood. He nodded. Anguish, both mental and physical took hold of him and he gripped his wrist gingerly. I told him to scat.

"He got up slowly with one hand. As he turned, I hit him on the back of his left shoulder with my cane for good measure. He tripped plunging face first with a shriek. He lay there for a moment, stunned, got up and stumbled away. He looked back at me in a justifiable rage. At that moment, I realized I might have gone a bit too far. At the end of the alley he turned and held up his good hand and gave me the finger, "Fuck you!" He yelled, "I'll get you. I'll get you good and that little bitch." He staggered across the street and disappeared.

"I shouldn't have hit him the second time, nor should I have hit him the third time, I know that, but he attempted to commit a most despicable crime. He needed to be taught a lesson. His face was bloodied. It looked as if someone smashed an over-ripe tomato on his nose. It was evident it was broken also."

"I looked around the alley, but the young woman was nowhere to be seen. The brick was still in its place, but the twenty had disappeared. I considered putting another twenty under it, but how would I know if she'd receive it and not some hooligan like the rapist. No, I straightened my coat and walked out of the alley. All the way home I felt invigorated, alive, like I did in the old days.

◆ ◆ ◆

Forty-two years in the Marine Corps has a tendency to make you feel invincible, but after two years of retirement this little action left my heart pounding. Yes, I was excited, I felt alive, but I was also trembling and experienced a bit of shortness of breath at the time.

I didn't mention the shortness of breath, nor the pounding heart. Miranda would have me in the E.R. within a minute fawning at me and yelling out orders to the nurses. At the start she appeared angry, though, I couldn't tell if it was at me or the cause of the encounter. As the story unfolded, I saw the fear that dominated her face turn to sadness. This I knew was for the young woman, for she always championed the downtrodden.

When I told her about the money and the lip balm, she laughed and said that was like me to think of something like giving her lip balm. But she also admonished me for taking the chance I did. I told her non-sense that I've handled more dangerous men in combat. She agreed with me, but said I wasn't young anymore and put her arms around me and kissed me on the cheek.

That night as I got into bed, I couldn't help but think of the young girl shivering in a cold alley. I will sleep in a warm, comfortable, safe bed with my wife and she will sleep in a cold box alone and in constant danger. It was a long time before I could shut my mind off and fall into a deep troubled sleep.

◆ ◆ ◆

The next night and the next and the next after that, I entered the alley at approximately the same time. The young girl was nowhere to be seen. On the fourth night with the weather worse than the first refuse blew in all directions, some rose up to almost two stories. Still the girl was not there. Again, I felt disappointed. I wanted to know if she was alright.

I wanted to help her, although, I have given the problem much thought, each solution seemed not enough and temporary. The idea of leaving or handing her twenty dollars a week just didn't seem enough, although it would make her life a little easier.

I couldn't ask her to come home with me. What would Miranda say? Anyway I was sure she would have no part of that, even though she did feel somewhat sad for the young woman. Do I call some type of social network, a church, perhaps? Would she even accept the help of a church or any government agency? No, if she would, she would've been in their care now instead of scrounging through garbage cans for food and sleeping in a box. Did she even know she needed help? Who in their right mind would want to live under these conditions? I thought for right now it would be better to give her money every so often. We had more than enough to keep us for the next fifty years, if we're careful. I found the brick and placed it inside the opening of her box and placed twenty under it.

I went to my warm home and told Miranda, sure she would scold me for putting myself into harm's way again, but at least I would know that I tried to help, if only a little.

I was wrong. Miranda hugged and kissed me on the cheek saying I was a good man. I smiled, happy in her adoration, until I thought of the young woman. How can I help her without her getting angry with me?

The next day turned even colder forecasting snow later in the evening and depending on who you listened to from one to four inches. Even an inch in the alley would make the young woman's life a misery. I ventured back to the alley that evening. The wind howled and shrieked to an ear piercing pitch. She was not there. Had she abandoned all her things? No, I'm sure she wouldn't do that. Did some tragedy befall her? My mind reached into scenarios I didn't want to believe. The twenty was gone, but the brick was still in the same spot, by the flap of her box.

I took twenty dollars out of my pocket and placed it under the brick. It flapped in the wind. I stood and gazed up at the lighted windows. The wind died suddenly and silence blanketed the alley and bits of refuse settled to the ground until the next gale would blow through.

I walked to the center of the intersection and looked out on the street, an occasional pedestrian walked by huddled in their long winter overcoats. Their scarves wrapped neatly around their necks, keeping out the frigid evening air. Hats pulled down partially covering their faces not looking left or right, just straight ahead. I remained statue still enjoying the windless atmosphere, no one noticed me and if they did, no one cared. Out of the corner of their eyes I might have been another homeless person, a shadow, a specter, someone to be looked at or through, but not really seen, someone not worth taking note of. This is how I felt the young woman must feel when walking through the streets. For the first time, I realized how insensitive I have been to these unfortunate souls. I too treated them like they weren't there. In some sense that's exactly how I felt in retirement. I was not needed. How sad that makes me feel. For forty years, I was someone, a force to be contended with. I was in charge, given duties that I faithfully and efficiently obeyed. Now...

Snowflakes descended, large fluffy and white. At first one or two slowly parachuted until they touch the cold hard ground waiting for others like it to build a cleansing blanket of white. The muffled sound of music and television shows bounced off the cold walls. I looked up and saw lights come on in the windows of the three different apartment buildings that made up this alley. Beyond the buildings the night sky appeared a very dark gray. Snowflakes plunged at an ever increasing rate with greater density. It's odd, how if you look straight up in the night air, they seem to come out of nowhere, to materialize in thin air. There was no wind and the flakes floated straight down in silence. If it was rain there would be an enormous clatter. I put my hand out with palm up and caught a crystallized water flake on the tip of a leathered finger. It did not take long for it to turn to a clear liquid and trickle off the edge. My coat soon became spotted with snow and then the spots turned to epaulets of white on my shoulders. My hair turned from gray to white, from dry to wet in no time, cold drops dripped down my back. I shivered.

I turned and looked at the empty box where the girl lived. I walked to it and placed the brick inside with the money under it and closed the four flaps. I made sure the tarp was secured and would not blow away in the wind. Maybe, the inside will stay dryer with them closed. I know her box will remain cold, no matter how much I closed it. I turned and left the alley.

I recounted my evening to my wife.

Miranda asked, "Have you given thought to what you would say to her if you two met again?"

I shrugged my shoulders and shook my head. That was actually a very good question. Leave it to Miranda to think of the important things. A flash exploded inside my head. I realized I should have thought of this. If I were on maneuvers I would have been able to plot each and every action to accomplish my goal. I would have anticipated everything that could have gone wrong and prepared for it. But retirement and idleness has fuddled my brain. Inactivity has rusted the iron cogs and wheels of my thought processes. Is this what I have to look forward to for the rest of my life? I realized I needed some type of job to scrape the cob-webs out of my head and not just feeding squirrels in the park. I will have to give this plenty of thought. In the meantime I'm not even sure if the young woman would ever listen to me. I haven't seen her and I'm not certain she was the one who took the money from the brick. I will have to make sure of that. That will be my number one objective, to find her and make sure she is all right. After our encounter, I will decide what to do next. I smiled. I had made the beginning of a plan, now to implement it.

◆ ◆ ◆

The next day at noon, my usual time, I ventured to the park down the street from our apartment building. Although it had stopped snowing, the sky remained a leaden color threatening more snow. The air remained bitter cold and I could feel the bite of it on my cheeks. The wind picked up and blew snow from the empty leafless tree branches; it reminded me of a snow globe.

Taking care not to slip on the icy sidewalk, I carefully stepped to a bench, brushed it off and sat down to feed peanuts to my furry friends. After two years of retirement, the boredom of civilian life was taking a toll on me. I really needed something to stimulate my mind and occupy my body, but what? When you are used to leading men into battle and suppressing an enemy in death to death war, what can you do when you retire? I'm too old to join the police force and being a guard is not to my liking, too sedentary.

Occasionally, I saw some acquaintance and nodded or said, 'hello.' I found, that I had nothing in common with most of the people in my building; they had a different mindset and they didn't experienced the trials and travails of life as I did. So for the most part I remained alone and silent. There's something sad about being silent and not interacting with other humans on a cold gray day. It's like standing on the sidelines of a football game that your team is being pummeled. You can't look away and can't offer any assistance. I wished Miranda had come out with me, but she hates the cold and sitting on a frozen park bench, well…

While I waited for the squirrels come and get their treats, I gave my dilemma some thought. Bits of snow fell from the trees and I looked up to see my friends scurrying across the frozen branches, as sure in their footing as if it were a summer's day. It seemed all color had disappeared, everything was one shade of gray or another, pewter, slate, silver or steel and any color there may have been appeared faded. It's like nothing's right or nothing's wrong, it just is.

One squirrel jumped down and adeptly landed on the iron fence across the sidewalk from me. It crouched there watching me with its tail undulating and hair fluttering in the breeze. I reached into my pocket and pulled out my bag of peanuts. I didn't notice anything but the squirrel. Holding tight to the bottom of the bag, I flicked it and half of the contents flew on the ground in front of the squirrel. It jumped off the fence and with quick quirky motions attacked the nuts nibbling as many as it could while casting wary eyes at anything that moved. Soon its friends scampered down to get their fair share.

I never liked wearing hats and felt my short cropped hair ruffle as the cold breeze rushed across my scalp. Lifting my collar and hunching my shoulders against the wind, I sprayed all the peanuts in front of me for the squirrels to pick up. Four more came scurrying down from the branches to get their portion of a noon meal. They seemed impervious to the cold, but at sixty-two, I was shivering, even with the heavy coat I wore. I decided to stay five more minutes then go home and have a hot cup of coffee and curl up with a good book.

My mind was so fixed on the squirrels; I didn't notice a shadow cross in front of me. Suddenly there was a pair of dirty athletic shoes on the sidewalk pointing in my direction. I looked up and there was the girl from the alley. I started.

She stood there frozen and with a scowl on her face. Her cold ice blue eyes glared at me as her hair was whipped by the wind. Both hands stuck in the pockets of her oversized filthy coat. She pulled her left hand out of her pocket. There were two crumpled up twenty dollar bills in it.

Two women from my building just happened to walk by. Both smiled in recognition nodding with prim expressions on their faces. They gazed at the girl and it was clear they did not like the looks of her and made a wide berth around her.

"I don't want to have sex with you," the young woman said with a voice seething with disgust.

The two women stopped, both horrified, but not speechless. "Well!" blurted out one of my neighbors with a gleeful expression of newly found juicy tid-bits to spread around. The other looked at me as if I were a molester of small children. She grabbed the arm of her friend and hurried her away, but not fast enough or far enough not to hear our discourse, but then the girl's voice rang out loud enough for the dead to hear.

"Stop leaving me money." The girl's voice increased both in intensity and anger. She wasn't paying attention to the women or didn't care if she embarrassing me. "I'm in trouble now because of you." Her voice was loud, determined and malignant.

I could hear the two women exclaim, "Oh my." The young woman held out the money that I left her in her hand. I couldn't move. My mind didn't comprehend what she was implicating. Me have sex with her? She's just a child and a scrawny one at that. Why would I jeopardize my life with Miranda for her? I sat there frozen, confused and angry.

She flicked the bills at me.

I opened my mouth to say something, but I was speechless.

The two women scurried on a few feet giving me scowls worse than the young girl's. Then both blurted out, "Pervert," in unison. While one continued, "Wait till I tell your wife."

"Mind your business you old bats," I yelled. I would ever stray from my wife, how dare they suggest that I would.

They looked insulted, "Well, I never," one said as she turned red hustling the two away.

"It's evident." I yelled in retort, satisfied that I finally had an outlet to tell those two nosy bitches to bug off. How dare they? What have I ever done to lead them to believe what the young girl was saying?

Three men, who occupied the next bench, laughed shaking their heads as they got up. "A little young, isn't she Sarge?" When they walked by us, one of the men turned and yelled, "Good luck Dick."

My face turned red hot and my scalp tingled. I was angry, no I was more than angry. I was volcanic. I hate being called 'Dick.' It's a name that would throw me into fits.

"And you three can just mind your own business," I commanded.

I turned to the young woman who embarrassed me in front of people who knew me and where I lived. People who I was sure would spread gossip about this encounter all over my apartment building by the time I got back. I would forever be looked upon as a child molester, even though I had no such intentions.

I bolted up, scowled and pointed my finger at my antagonist like I was about to skewer her. Her features changed from one of anger to fright. I stood there stammering. She recoiled.

"Take your sex money back," she screamed. "All you men are alike. You think because a young girl is in trouble, you can shower them with a few dollars for a fuck or blow-job."

I couldn't believe what I just heard. I sputtered. I imagine looking back on it now, it would seem funny, but then it wasn't.

Her eyes took on a shine as tears gathered behind her eyelashes. I could hear the anguish in her voice. At any other time my anger would have melted, but not now, she stabbed me hard with her accusation.

"Do you think that is what this is about?" I found it hard to control my temper. "That I want to have sex with a scrawny pre-teenage iti-bity of a girl." I could see she had taken affront by that statement. She cringed and withdrew a little more. I couldn't stop, I went for the jugular. "One who scrounges through garbage and smells like the dead?" I bellowed with indignation. She truly seemed hurt. I should have turned and left, but instead I continued, although, my anger abated by the sting that I inflicted upon her and her penitent expression. Pointing to the money on the ground, "That is not why I left you the money," I said. "I thought I was helping you. I thought you might appreciate someone giving you a helping hand." I reached forward to show my willingness to forgive and forget.

She recoiled and her anger flared. "Helping hands never come free," she screamed. By now tears streamed from her eyes. "They always come with attachments and commitments. And I'll…"

I threw out my hand to her to stop her rant and shook my finger, "If you do not want my help, fine. But you certainly didn't say for me to mind my business the other night when that hoodlum attacked you."

Her eyes glared in defiance. I could tell she is not one to be trifled with. She puckered her lips, angrily shook her head and shouted, "I didn't need your help then and I don't need it now. I don't want your help and I will never want it." She scrunched up her face, saluted me with a middle finger and stormed off. After five steps she turned around and screamed, "Leave me alone."

"Fine," I bellowed and stormed off in the opposite direction.

She took three more steps and turned again. "Fine!" She screamed.

I turned back toward her and retorted, "Fine." I was determined to get in the last word. Kicking at anything in my way, I stomped toward the end of the park. I was in such a rage I didn't realize that I was walking in the opposite direction of my apartment building. I didn't care, as long as I didn't go in her direction. The money probably blew away in the wind. I didn't look back to see if the girl or anyone else picked it up. I was angry. My face felt hot in the cold air. I stomped off as fast as I could. Crunch, crunch was all I heard on the hard snow and ice. I needed to expel the anger. *If she wants me to leave her alone, well by God, I will.*

I finally made it home and told Miranda of my encounter with the young woman.

"Well, Richard you really can't blame her, now can you, after all she probably gets propositioned all the time." She laughed so hard tears leaked from the corners of her eyes.

Angry that she found my embarrassment so funny, I gave her my sternest look.

She saw my anger rising and the hurt expression on my face. Her laughing stopped and she tilted her head and gave me a sad smile. "Look Richard," she said sympathetically. "I'm not laughing at you to be mean." Her smile returned, "it's just sometimes you can be so…"

My anger again reached a boiling point and I began to walk in angry circles. But, I couldn't tell if I was angry at myself for not seeing what Miranda saw right away, or if I was mad at her for being right, again. *God! She's always right.* I glared at her, huffed and then went into the bedroom slamming the door shut.

After a while, I calmed down. Miranda was sitting on the sofa with a magazine on her lap lightly humming a tune that was on the radio.

"I'm sorry," I said contritely. "I didn't mean to fly off the handle. When I look at that woman all I see is our daughter. I can't imagine her being thrown out on the street to fend for herself in this city." I sat down beside her. "It's just… I just wanted to help this woman. Handing her a few dollars is all I could think to do." I could feel my temperature rising again at the thought of being rejected. *That's what it was. I never felt that before.* "And all she did accuse me of exploiting her circumstance."

"Gunny, you need to sit down, calmly talk to this woman and explain everything, in a calm and sensible way, if you really want to help her." She put the magazine on the coffee table and rubbed my arm. "Unfortunately, I don't think she'll get closer than a hundred feet of you. Too bad there wasn't a way I could be there." A moment later, Miranda snapped her fingers and she had this devilish look in her eyes. "Why don't both of us look for her together," she said giving me a smile and pinched my cheek. "I'm actually really curious," she said coyly. "I want to see my competition."

I looked at her surprised, "It would be a good idea if you were with me. Maybe we could look for her tomorrow evening." I started to form a plan of action. "And you don't have to worry about competition. You have me lock, stock, and barrel."

She turned her head toward me, brushed my cheek with her fingers and gave me a look that said it all. 'I know.'

CHAPTER THREE

ADDISON KNEW SHE HAD MADE A MISTAKE. She realized from the start that the old man wasn't like the others who tried to proposition her. But she let her temper and independence get in her way. She ran from the park and huddled in a narrow doorway waiting for the man come by. She wanted to say she was sorry and that she really appreciated the gesture, but he never did. She supposed he was walking off his anger.

After a few minutes she went back into the park and found the money skittering from bush to bush, picked it up and made a resolution to hand it back politely.

She scurried across the street and hurried to her alley. On the way she decided to get a sandwich a McDonald's. She entered the restaurant and was the fourth person in line. The guy in front of her turned around, looked down at her and inspected the source of the rancid smell. She looked at him red faced and backed up a step. He crinkled his nose and started to gag. Covering his mouth he got out of line and walked to the door. As he left, her eyes followed him. At the door he turned staring directly at her and shook his head. Addison felt numb. She had experienced eye rolling, head shaking and sometimes gagging, but for some reason, at this moment, it really stung.

The woman in front turned and started to say in a loud high-pitched voice, "something stin..." She stopped when she turned and saw Addison.

Addison's lip trembled. She eyed the woman, turned around and hurriedly walked out holding back her tears.

On the way out someone shouted, "There should be a sign, 'No stinky people,' and he and a few other patrons laughed. Addison felt overwhelming despair. Their laughter hurt worse this time than any other time she had experienced people's ridicule. Maybe it was because of the argument with the old man and his biting words. Maybe because she was at the end of her rope and she knew she was in trouble, both physically and mentally. She ran back to her temporary home and crawled into her box and cried. She did not leave it until the next day.

◆ ◆ ◆

The next day at noon, I journeyed to the park again. However, I considered picking another spot to feed the squirrels, but that bench was special. I had met my wife while sitting on that it forty years ago. I would never allow anyone, for any reason, to push me off of it. The sun was a little warmer turning the snow to slush. Cold drops fell like bombs from the branches sending out rings of water in the puddles in which they landed. Brown earth and green grass peeked through the snow in all the areas except where it was deepest. I really couldn't get the young girl out of my mind. Yes, she angered me to an extent that I wanted to say the hell with her and cast her aside, but how many times has she had that happen to her? I knew if Miranda and I could sit her down and talk to her, we could arrive at a solution.

Scampering out of the way of passersby my gray haired friends scurried around with tails trailing trying to snatch whatever they could. Soon, my supply of peanuts was depleted, I was about to go home when a figure sat down beside me. I turned my head and was taken totally by surprise and shock. It was the young girl. Was she here to make me feel more the fool than I already felt? I didn't think so or she wouldn't have sat down next to me. She looked as though she scrubbed her face and I could see her hands were only dirty around the nails. She glanced at me. Judging from her expressions, she was experiencing some internal war with her emotions, changing from fright to curiosity and then contrition.

"I'm sorry for acting like a fool yesterday," she mumbled. Her chin buried deep in the collar of her coat. She folded her hands onto her lap, fingers wrenching each other in nervousness. "It's just that, I've been approached by all kinds of men thinking I'm homeless and would be happy to give them a blow job for a few dollars."

My head jerked back and I raised my eyebrows in shock, did I just hear her use such vulgarity out in the open? Is she in the habit of communicating like this all the time?

"Or throw them a fuck for a few bucks."

I wanted to wash her mouth out with soap. I couldn't fathom such a young girl talking like that. My daughter would never think of doing such a thing. I could feel my face flush with combination of embarrassment and anger.

Maybe I had misjudged this girl and she was actually deranged.

She looked at me with fierce eyes as anger gripped her voice, "Well, I won't; I would rather starve to death than submit to that." Her facial features softened. "I don't like to swear, but I use it to prove a point." She smiled at the look of relief on my face. "Shocked you, didn't it?"

I chuckled nodding, "I must say it did coming from one as young as you."

She gave me a curious look, "Don't you talk to teenagers or you haven't noticed that they use that kind of language all the time."

I started to laugh, "I have to say, except for the last two years, I haven't been around civilians, at least Americans." I sighed, "And these last few years I've been at grips trying to cope with retirement and haven't paid much attention to much else."

I found it interesting that I just confessed my dilemma to a young stranger and one who was homeless and in worse condition than myself. I found it absurd that she would care about my plight when she struggles with her basic needs. "I'm sorry if men proposition you. I would be angry in your shoes," I said.

My guard was completely shattered and I found that I was enjoying myself talking to this young orphan. At least I thought of her as one, for what parent would cast her out.

"You're forgiven for yesterday," I said. "Maybe I should have handled it differently and not storm off. I should have explained my intentions more clearly and calmly."

She sat there staring at me for a moment. I wondered

what she was thinking about. Her eyes kept changing from ice blue to silver depending upon the light filtering through the clouds. Neither of us said a word or took our eyes off each other. A stiff breeze blew in from the east and with it I realized how bad she smelled. I wanted to get up and sit on the upwind side of her, but I was afraid that would embarrass her and she would walk away. She pulled her coat tighter around her neck. I could tell she was gauging me and trying to make up her mind.

"Why do you keep leaving me money?" Anger and resentment entered her tone of voice again. "Nothing's for free. What do you want?" Her last inquiry edged with suspicion.

"I'm sorry if it offends you." My voice took a mellow tone. "Do you want me to stop leaving you money?"

"Yes!" she said defiantly. "No," she paused for a second and then whined, "I don't know." Her knuckles cracked from her wringing her hands.

The squirrels having finished the nuts I threw on the ground scurried about chasing each other. She smiled at them. I realized that they didn't run back up into the trees when she approached.

"Sometimes," She said in a low voice, "I get to buy peanuts and I feed the squirrels here." She pointed to a squirrel in the crook of tree, "That one I call 'Rebel' because he's all gray and refuses to come near me. The others though will if I hold out a peanut." She looked at me and a small smile broke out on her face. We shared a common interest.

"How do you get money to buy peanuts?" I asked.

"Bottles and cans," she replied giving a look of 'Duh.'

I realized my stupidity and turned red. "Of course," I said.

Her facial features changed every second. I could tell she wasn't unstable like so many of the other homeless. I could also see she was struggling to decide if she trusted me or not. I felt she wanted to, but found it hard to let her guard down. Maybe she has been out on the street too long to trust anyone anymore.

"Look young lady, I assure you, I have no ulterior motives. I just want to help and leaving you a few dollars once in a while is the only way I know." I adjusted my body on the bench to face her.

She would be quite pretty if she were clean and had decent clothes to wear. She stuck her hands in her pocket and I saw her shiver a little despite the warmth of the afternoon. I wondered if she was sick. She pulled one hand out of her pocket and wiped her sleeve across her nose.

She stared at me with a curious look. "Why me? Why not help one of the old people who live on the street?" Defiance appeared on her face again. Clouds moved slowly in the afternoon sky opening the sun's light directly into her face. Icy eyes squinted at me. It reminded me of the antagonists in old westerns before a shootout.

Rubbing my finger across my lips, I gave it some thought. "It's because your youth shocked me." I decided truth was my best option. "You are too young to be out here." I waved my hand to indicate the streets. "Maybe I am used to seeing all the other homeless and like most other people like me feel like they are just part of the landscape. But you," I pointed my gloved finger, "you shocked me. I have never been so moved as to that first time I saw you. Or angered at the last time," I gave her a big smile. "At first, I thought you were older. Then when you took a step backwards under the light... I thought about it many times. Even if the person I saw that first moment was older, I still would have given them some money, but I have to admit that would be as far as I would've gone. I would never have gone back to the alley looking for them."

"But why do you continue? What are your motives?" Her question had an edge of desperation.

I slowly shook my head and held out my hands, "I have no motives, other than to help you."

"Everybody has motives," she said testily.

"Well then, maybe my motive is a reward in heaven. At my age, one starts to think of such things. I have done many things in my life that can be construed as unforgivable, most of them need atonement," a smile crossed my face. "Although, I'm pretty sure God would see through that ruse and know I was just trying to make up for past transgressions."

She turned her head and watched at the squirrels scamper across the barren branches. She wore socks with the toes cut out on her hands which she rubbed vigorously and blew on her bare fingers, then tucked them in her pockets. Her hands were clean, but her fingernails were broken and crusted in dirt. I saw a slight shiver and her nose was running again. I pulled out a clean handkerchief and gave it to her. She wiped her nose and made to give it back. I shook my head. "You keep it, I have plenty more." I noticed the joints in her fingers were cracked from the cold I imagined. "Those socks don't look very warming, would you like my gloves?"

"No," she shook her head, "Thank you for offering. If someone were to see them, they would take them from me. I don't want to take the chance. I need to keep a low profile from people like Max; he is the guy you saved me from." She turned her head toward me, shame written on her face. "Thank you for helping," she truly sounded grateful, "and for the money, it's really nice of you." She no longer had anger in her eyes. In them was pain, hurt and embarrassment. Wind had picked up buffeting the hair sticking out from under her hat. "I should really be going. If I'm gone from the alley too long someone will take my place or steal my stuff."

Reaching into my pocket, "Can I give you a few dollars?"

"No, thanks anyway, I still have some from the first time." She stood up and put her hand in her pocket and pulled it right out. "I also picked these up off the ground yesterday. It's yours take it," she extended her hand. In it was the money she threw at me. When I didn't take it she extended her hand further, "If people find it on me they'll take it and it will give them a reason for taking more," her face turned red and tears welled in her eyes. I realized, despite her strong persona, how vulnerable she was on the street. I reached for the money with my left hand. "I don't want to give them anything." She turned and started to walk away hands in her pockets and her head tucked into her coat.

After she walked ten feet away, "Wait," I shouted,

"What is your name?" I didn't want to end our conversation. I wanted to know all about this wayward child. The how and why she decided to live on the street. She didn't seem to be demented, or racked by drug abuse or alcoholism. She seemed normal, except for her situation.

"Addy, Addison." She smiled.

"I'm Richard Cramer." I continued trying to extend our conversation, "I don't like Rick or Rich and most certainly not Dick, Richard is preferred or if you want 'Gunny', in fact that is what all my friends call me." I stood and walked toward her and held out my hand to her.

She looked around and hesitantly extended her hand. She had a strong grip for such a small young woman. I noticed, as I shook her hand, it was rough and bony and her cheeks were hallowed. Even though her coat added much bulk to her appearance, this young woman is emaciated.

"It's nice to meet you Richard."

I smiled as she walked away. It was five days before Thanksgiving. I sat down thinking about our encounter. Relieved, yet distraught about the appearance of Addison, it made me more determined to help her, but how? Shadows disappeared as the sky clouded over. A brisk wind began to blow and the temperature dropped at least ten degrees. I got up from the bench and walked pensively to my apartment.

◆ ◆ ◆

Yesterday Max stood in a doorway of an apartment building across from one of the parks in this section of town. He had been following the little bitch from the alley and saw her walk up to the old man and started to scream at him. He could hear her voice plain as day, but not what she was saying. And from the sound of the man's response he was in the same frame of mind. He saw the two old ladies shaking their heads and walk away. He saw them turn toward the two arguers and say something only to scurry away in a huff, yak-ka-te yakking with animated body language twisting facial features all the way across the street. Max watched the three young men on the bench next to the old man get up laughing and joking at the two as they moved down to a more peaceful part of the park. He stood flat against the wall in the shadow of a doorway hidden from Addison that day as she stormed by him angrily cursing the old man. He knew if he confronted her that day she would want to take out her anger on him and he wasn't in a position or mood for that.

Now today, Max caught Addison walking down the block again and decided to follow her at a safe distance. Taking care not to be seen, he kept ducking into doorways and peeking out to keep track of her. He followed her toward the same park. As she crossed the street, he hid in an entryway of the same apartment building. Peeking around the edge of the alcove, Max watched as she sat down next to the old man.

He wasn't paying attention to anything but the two people in the park when the door to the apartment building opened and an old woman came out. She ordered Max to leave. This was no place for a bum to stand out of the wind. Respectable people lived here and they don't need to have a smelly hobo stink up their entry way. If he didn't leave she would show him just how hard she could hit him with her cane.

"What the hell is it with you old people and your canes?" He said as he tried to ignore her. He wanted to see what was going to happen in the park and if the 'Bitch' was going to cause another scene.

"I said git," bellowed the woman poking Max with the end of her cane, each time a little harder and each time a little closer to his face.

"All right, All right," he pleaded. When he didn't move fast enough she slapped the cane on his wrist. Even through the cast, pain shot through him like a hot knife through butter spiraling up the rest of his arm. Max jerked his arm back and made like he was going to hit her.

"You go ahead, I'll scream bloody murder," the old woman threatened. "You'll be in jail faster than you can sneeze." There was a satisfying smirk on her face. "Now get the hell off of my stoop," she bellowed raising her cane.

"All right, just stop poking me with your muther-fukin cane," he cried.

He carefully stepped out of the doorway into dimming sunlight. When he turned back to the scene in the park, both the old man and Addison were standing about ten feet apart. She walked back to him and stood for a moment and then extended her hand. *The Bitch just got more money.* Addison put her hands in her pocket, turned and walked out of the park away from where Max stood. The old man seemed to be coming his way. Max didn't want him to know that he was keeping tabs on them, so he rushed down the sidewalk mixing in with the crowd and turned at the corner. Max decided to go home, at least what he called home and get out of the cold. On his way home, he thought that their time was coming. He would square things with those two, especially the bitch. *Bitch, she's gittin rich off the old man. Well, the next time I see her we'll see. I make sure I get some of it.*

CHAPTER FOUR

BY THE TIME I ENTERED MY BUILDING, the first few flakes descended to the ground at an angle. I had made a decision. I wanted to run it by Miranda. After the door was closed, I tucked my gloves into my coat pockets and hung my coat in the hall closet. "Miranda," I called.

"In here dear, I'm talking to Elizabeth on the phone." She gave me a concerned look as I entered the living room, "Is there something wrong?"

"No," I said in an off-handed way, trying not to sound excited. "I just want to talk to you about something, but it can wait. Tell Elizabeth I miss her and I will call her later." Miranda gave me a puzzled look. I walked over to the big living-room window, moisture covered the bottom half. In the distance, I watched the snow start to fall in earnest clouding the buildings across the park in a grayish mist. *Addison will have a cold night tonight.* The street noises were muffled and the colors blurred.

"Honey," Miranda spoke into the phone. There was a slight edge to her voice. "Can we call you back later, O.K.? Thank you. Yes, love you too. Give my granddaughter a kiss for me. Bye." I heard the click of the phone hanging up. "Now," she said concerned, "what's so important Richard?"

"Nothing's important." It always amazed me that she could read me like a book.

"Non-sense, you practically told me to get off the phone," she said pointedly. "Since when did you ever delay talking to your daughter? And whenever you look out the window with your hands behind your back, something's on your mind. Now out with it," she demanded. I heard her settle back on the couch with her arms folded across her chest, her right eyebrow raised in an arch while she waited for me to start with an amused look on her face. I didn't have to see it, after so many years of marriage, I knew.

I turned around and faced her, "I told you about the girl I saw scrounging in garbage cans," Miranda nodded slowly. "The one..."

"This is the one in the park yesterday?" I nodded. Miranda moved to the edge of the sofa with her hands in her lap and a smile appeared and her eyes twinkled. "This is the girl who accused you of wanting to have sex with her. The same one who threw your lust money back at you?" I nodded. "The very same one Audrey Meddleson more than hinted that you were having an affair with?"

The amusement in her voice pinched me, but I nodded feeling my temperature rise. I didn't need to be reminded of how embarrassed I felt. "Yes." I said curtly, "While, I was at the park today, she came over to me and sat down next to me."

"Oh?" Surprise and curiosity crossed her face, but she still had a sparkle in her eyes.

The room was warm when I came in a few minutes ago, but now, it seemed overly hot. Maybe it was just me worrying what Miranda would say. Maybe it was me feeling foolish. Maybe it was me feeling sad that again here I'm in a warm apartment and Addison will be sleeping in a box in the cold. "I know you are going to say that she's playing me," I sat down in a chair facing her. "I'm a fairly good judge of character and I don't think she's like that." Miranda started to interrupt me, but I held up my hand. "I offered her money today, but she turned me down, in fact, she handed me the money she threw at me yesterday." I dug into my pocket and produced the two twenty dollar bills, crinkled and slightly soiled. "She said, she had more than enough left from what I gave her the first time. Her hands were freezing, so I offered her my gloves and again she turned me down. Addison, that's her name, was afraid someone might steal them."

Miranda settled back down on the sofa. Fingers of her left hand pinched her lower lip, her left elbow being supported by her right arm. A position she always takes when a problem comes up and she has to figure out a solution.

"I know," I continued, "I may seem foolish, but..."

"No dear, actually, I'm glad that you brought this up." She got off the sofa and came over and sat on my lap and put her arms around me, I did the same to her. "You have been mumbling about homeless people ever since you saw this girl. I know you want to help this, Addison, right?" I nodded my head. "Well, how can we help her? Have you thought of that?"

"We?" I asked surprised and shook my head. "I don't even know if she wants to be helped. She didn't want any more money. And she seemed kind of hesitant to be around me. She also seems to be very independent and too head-strong for a young girl in her predicament."

"That's because you are a man and a woman needs to be leery around them, especially someone that young. Let's give this some thought and at dinner tonight we will toss some ideas together and see if we can come up with a solution." Miranda nuzzled up to me and kissed my neck. "I can understand why she would be hesitant around you. Why she wouldn't want to trust herself around you."

I looked in her eyes. Her expression made me feel wanted and loved. I smiled. "Really?" She smiled nodding. She got up, grabbed my hand and pulled me into the bedroom. I followed her thinking how lucky I was to have a woman like her.

◆ ◆ ◆

Before Miranda was to start dinner, she said, "Let's go out to eat. We haven't gone out in a long time."

I nodded, "That's a splendid idea." It had been a few weeks since we went out and I thought it would be delightful to sit in a cozy corner of a restaurant, just the two of us enjoying each other's company. The snow had stopped and it's a short walk to her favorite restaurant. I had a feeling she had an ulterior motive. The restaurant was on the other side of the alley, two doors down from the pub I frequented.

I helped her with her coat and we took the elevator down to the street. It was approximately six o'clock when we exited our building into a cacophony of cars horns, sirens, revving engines and other sounds of rush hour traffic. The sidewalks were crowded with people going about their business. All huddled in their long over coats, scarves and hats. Miranda and I walked slowly arm in arm chatting about our daughter Elizabeth. When we arrived at the alley, she stopped suddenly.

"Is this where the girl lives?" I nodded. She looked down the alley curiously careening her neck, so she could get a look at this mysterious girl. "Where's the box?"

"Down at the end of the alley to the left."

"Let's go see if she is there," she said enthusiastically and started off down the alley pulling me down with her. We walked slowly, her hand tucked neatly under my arm. Snow covered the ground hiding the refuse and smells that alleys accumulated. We could hear the sound of music and televisions coming from the apartments above. Almost all the lights from the windows emitted a dull glow behind old shades lighting the inside of the alley and all of the corners. Addison's box was opened. She was not inside.

Miranda looked at me questioningly. Her mouth was down-turned in disappointment and sorrow shown in her eyes. I shrugged my shoulders. I also felt disappointed. I wanted Miranda and her to meet. It would also give Addison the peace of mind and show her that I did not mean her any harm. I took twenty dollars out of my pocket and placed it inside her box then we walked out.

"How will we get hold of her?" Miranda asked as we walked away.

Again, I shrugged my shoulders, "I guess she'll find me, if she wants to, probably at the park."

We went to dinner. Our conversation was a little subdued both of us were disappointed Addison was not in her box. After we paid our bill, we walked by the alley on the way home. We hesitated at the entrance, but did not go inside. The money would be enough of a calling card if she wanted to talk to me. When we got home, we discussed our plans for the next day. I as usual would sit on a park bench and feed the squirrels. Miranda had business at the hospital, where she volunteered, early in the morning.

◆ ◆ ◆

The next day, about noon, I again sat on a cold park bench. The squirrels found me and waited for their supply of peanuts. Only this time the sidewalks were still covered with snow from the night before and the tree branches wore a white coating over them. The fence across from where I sat was also covered with white fluffy patches except where the birds and squirrels made their tracks.

I spread the peanuts out on the ground on the other side of the fence. The snow was a couple of inches deep, so the squirrels had to hop to reach the nuts. I stood, wondering if Addison would come and see me when I felt a presence next to me. Turning my head, I smiled, "Well, hello Addison." The money I left her worked. I had the feeling she would contact me if I left her more money.

Her hands were in her pockets and she gave me an irritated look. Pulling her left hand, "I don't need this," she said curtly. In her hand, the twenty I left her last night sticking out of her fingers.

"I had the feeling you would say that," I said a little amused. "Think of it as a calling card." She held the money out to me. When I wouldn't take it she pushed it toward me.

"I can't take that," I said holding my hands up. "My wife would be angry with me, it was she who insisted. We went to the alley, she wanted to meet you."

Her face showed confusion, "You're married?"

"Yes," I smiled, she was surprised. "Forty years. Miranda, my wife, thought if I left you the money, you would contact me, so you see, I couldn't possibly take it back." I could see her facial expression change. It seemed to show a slight sense of relief. "Didn't I mention that I'm married yesterday?" She shook her head. "Sorry, it must have slipped my mind, that's what happens as one gets older. You have a tendency to misplace things and thoughts."

One of the squirrels jumped up onto the fence, pushing off the tuft of snow and stood hovering on its hind legs. I chuckled and took out a peanut and held it in my hand for it to grab. It hesitated looking from me to Addison and back. She took the peanut from my fingers and held it out to the squirrel. I turned to see her face. She smiled, her eyes shined brightly. I felt an overwhelming sense of respect for this young woman at that moment. Here she was homeless, living in a box and still she had compassion for animals in need. The squirrel reached out and took the peanut then scurried away. Addison turned her head toward me and just looked.

"Addison, come home with me." My face flushed with prickly heat all over. I couldn't believe I just said that. It came out in a rush, even before I knew I was going to ask her. What would Miranda say if I just showed up with Addison in tow? I tried to sound like it would be all right, after all I couldn't retract it.

"I'm sure Miranda would want me to ask you." I said praying she would say no.

"No, I can't," she said hesitantly.

"Yes you can," a voice intoned. There stood Miranda. I was so focused on Addison, that I didn't see Miranda walk up to us. "Addison, I'm Miranda, Richard's wife and we both would like you to come to our house. If for nothing else than to get out of this damn cold," Miranda slinked up to me grabbing my arm.

Addison looked confused, torn apart. She shook her head, "I can't. Thank you anyway." Sadness filled her voice.

"Look, it's almost Thanksgiving. If not today, you're welcome to have a holiday dinner with us. You shouldn't be out here all by yourself, especially during the holidays." I took off my glove and reached into my wallet for a card. I handed it to her. "Don't say no, think about it." I leaned over and looked into her eyes. She backed away a step. Tears welled into the corners of her lashes. "If you change your mind, just come over. We'll have a place already set for you, in case."

"Please, Addison, think about it." Miranda extended her hand to Addison's shoulder. Addison moved back a little further. Miranda took it all in stride. "If you don't, I'll be stuck listening to Gunny's wartime stories." Miranda playfully winced.

Addison nodded, turned and ran out of the park, my card still clutched in her hand. Miranda and I looked at each other in helpless misery then slowly walked home in silence, arm in arm. Miranda put her head on my shoulder. She rubbed my arm.

CHAPTER FIVE

ADDISON HURRIED TOWARD 'HER' ALLEY, tears streamed down her face. People stared at her as she ran by, some with concern others with distaste. She paid no attention to them and let their muffled comments roll off her like rain on a duck's back. She ran past the Cramer's apartment and stopped at the corner.

She liked Richard. After all he fed the squirrels in the park. Anyone who would do that couldn't be all bad. She decided quickly that she liked Richard's wife also, it was her motherly demeanor something she missed and yearned. She had a kind face and her eyes conveyed warmth and caring. So why was she so hesitant on taking their offer?

"Because they will want me to change, everyone does," she said out loud as anger seeped into her consciousness. "Damn it," she hissed. She stood and leaned against the window of a corner store. Her breath came out in ragged gasps. Sweat leaked from her under her hat onto her forehead. She felt a sudden chill. Addison gazed at the card Richard gave her. MGySg Richard Cramer, USMC retired. There was a telephone number and an address. She stared at the words and the emblem of a golden globe and anchor. Her breath returned to normal as she peered down the street.

She watched Richard and Miranda walk up the street. She watched them in huddled conversation and wondered if they were talking about her. *People like that have more important things to talk about than me.* She watched as Miranda put her head on Richard's shoulder and imagine the love they felt for each other. She hoped she would someday find someone to love her like that. She watched the two disappear into the building. Addison slowly shook her head, *no one will.* Holding up the card in her hand Addison gave it one last look and slid the card deep in her pocket and began walking again.

She almost got to her alley when a hand reached out and grabbed her arm. She spun around, ready to hit whoever it was while sliding her hand into a pocket for her knife.

The hand belonged to Max.

"We got unfinished business Ad-di-son," he said in a nasally voice. "You and me gonna talk."

Max stepped out from the doorway of an apartment building. Addison saw the cast on his wrist secured to chest with a sling and a grimy bandage on his nose.

She looked down at his hand holding her arm. "Leave me alone," she hissed. She yanked her arm from his grip backing away.

He reached out, latching onto her sleeve with a vice-like grip. Looming over her, he let go of her sleeve and with surprising speed pinched her face hard with his nails digging gouges into her cheeks. People walking by looked away. They had no need to get involved in the affairs of two vagrants.

"Like I said," he hissed. "You and I got unfinished

business," his nails dug deeper causing Addison to cry out. He spun her around so her back was against the building. He looked around at the passersby to see if anyone would interfere, but none did. His grin exuded maliciousness as his gaze went from the fear in her eyes to her chest giving her a message of intent. "I intend to collect what's due me."

She tried to pull away but his fingers dug deeper. He slid his hand down to her neck. Panic flooded her mind as the image of the night when he tried to rape her took over her mind. Both hands flew up to her neck trying to dislodge his hand but he squeezed harder. His fingernails biting into her skin was like a cold bucket of water changing her mindset from being a victim to a victor. Her eyes lifted to his nose and the bandage that wrapped itself over the bridge. Their eyes met and she saw he thought he was in power of her. Her downturned mouth straightened and then turned into a smile. She saw first confusion and then incomprehension as she lowered her eyes back to his nose. She raised her hand and pinched and twisted it. Max howled. She went for his broken wrist.

◆ ◆ ◆

Delighted that he was causing her pain, but in seconds his expression turned to confusion. He followed her eyes to his nose and the realization of her next move became evident. He let go of her, but it was too late. Addison grabbed his nose and squeezed twisting as hard as she could. She then grabbed his wrist and yanked. Intense pain shot through his arm as he screamed and fell to his knees. She didn't stop twisting until he was on his back on the sidewalk writhing. He looked up at her just in time to see her foot kick him hard in the side. He bent into a fetal position and cried. She bent down and squeezed his nose again. Max screamed harder. Passersby stopped on the sidewalk, some laughed others glared at the two in disgust. He felt his pants grow wet.

Addison stood up and ran for all she was worth. After a few steps, she turned and saw Max with his knees curled to his chest crying. He held his broken hand in his other. People gave him a wide berth as they walked by him with distasteful leers. Addison held up her hand and gave him a finger and began running again. Addison laughed. Not at Max's pain, but at the feeling of victory. It made her feel like she was in charge of her life again. She had set herself free.

Max watched her disappear in the crowded sidewalk. He couldn't follow her, the pain in his wrist made him wretch all over the sidewalk. People walking by made rude comments about being drunk on the sidewalk in the middle of the day. After a minute he wiped his mouth with his sleeve. It took him a few minutes to get to his feet and then to be able to stand without holding on to the wall. Nodding toward the direction Addison ran, he said under his breath, "You're going to pay."

Max was about to leave, when he felt something hit him on the back.

"Look what you do to my sidewalk," yelled an angry Chinese woman. She hit him again with the business end of a broom. "Who going to clean?" She screamed pointing to the mess he made and began hitting Max again and again.

Max raised his good arm for protection but it was no

use, she kept pummeling him. As she hit him, she got madder and madder, spewing out words he could only imagine the meaning of. It's not that it hurt, because it didn't. It was that here again another old woman was beating him up. He tried to scurry away, but she kept it up following him until he ran off the sidewalk and into the street, where he was almost hit by a taxi.

"Bitch, I'm going to get you too." He screamed and hurried down the street.

◆ ◆ ◆

Addison knew not to go 'home' yet, just in case Max followed her. In fact, she thought it might be wise to look for another place to lay her head for the night and maybe look for a new place, she would retrieve her blanket later. Her cheeks stilled burned from Max's pinch and she rubbed them, slight trace of blood came off onto her fingers.

She still had a few dollars left of the money Richard had given her, so she decided to get a hot cup of coffee and maybe a pastry, if she had enough. Her stomach was grumbling. *I guess all the running and Max made me hungry.* As she was going into a local coffee shop, she held the door open for four teens like her leaving. *No, they weren't like her. They were normal, with normal lives.* They all snickered as they walked by her, the last one held her nose making a stinky face. Addison fumed, but didn't say anything.

She walked to the counter, ordered a large coffee and a pastry. Digging deep into her pocket, she pulled out the last of her money. Two dollars and some change. She decided she would have to forgo the pastry and asked to use the bathroom. She washed the blood off and some of the grime off her face and hands. Picking a table in the corner by the window away from everyone else, Addison watched life go by. People hurried left and right, heads somewhat bowed in the wind. Not one looking up, they walked by some invisible radar. She looked at their faces all clean and probably smelling like perfume or soap. Some toted briefcases or packages. Others carried nothing at all and had their clean hands stuffed in clean coat pockets with scarves wrapped around their necks. Their coats actually fit them, not some cast off as hers was, found in a dumpster smelling of garbage and who knew what else. She'd gotten used to the smell, but no one else did. She sipped her coffee and watched the lights turning on in the darkening sky. She sat there for two hours, alone and lonely.

The guy behind the counter walked over to her with one hand behind his back, the other held another cup of coffee. He looked down at her. The beginning of a smile appeared.

"I thought yours might be getting cold," he said with a hint of sympathy. "So I brought you a fresh one." He swung his hidden arm out, it held a muffin in it. "I thought you might like to have a muffin."

"I don't have the mon…"

He held his hand out, "Don't worry about it." He turned and started for the counter.

She looked up at him and smiled gloomily. "Thank you, I'll leave in a minute. It's just so warm in here."

He wasn't angry like most coffee shop workers were. He didn't grimace standing over her like many people do who show their displeasure. Addison wondered why he was being kind to her when the world seem to want her gone.

"Take your time. We're not busy. We're open all night." The guy turned and walked back to the counter to wait on a customer that just entered.

Not everyone is a jerk. She continued to watch people return home from work with her hands wrapped around the hot cup. *Home...* She sighed.

Addison waited in the coffee shop for another hour. She thanked the guy and even tried to give him a tip, she had two quarters left, which he adamantly refused.

◆ ◆ ◆

Standing in the doorway across the street from the alley, Addison scanned the neighborhood looking for Max. He wasn't anywhere to be seen.

I'm going to have to find a heavy stick, something to mash his wrist if he tries to attack me again. She smiled. *No, his nose.* Her smile broadened.

Addison entered the alley, keeping to one side, scanning any place someone might lay in wait. As she slunk by Mr. Lim's door, it opened and two men walked out carrying garbage cans.

They glared at her. She could tell by their expressions they didn't want her here. She sneaked by without saying a word and headed for her box. Before she entered, she kicked it hard. It moved about eight inches. *Good.*

She crawled inside and closed the flaps. Pulling out her knife, she found it the day after the attack and held it in her hand. After throwing the moving pad over her, she went to sleep.

✦ ✦ ✦

The pain in Max's wrist radiated into his brain causing him to see white spots before his eyes. He couldn't wait to get back to his hole to take one or two of the pains pills from his scrip. Stepping off the curb across the street from an abandoned building where he squatted, a hand grabbed his arm and jerked him backwards almost flipping him on his back. The image of the old man flashed through his mind as he shrieked. As he was falling back a car sped right by him horn blaring. He was seconds away from him being a splat on a windshield.

"Are you trying to get yourself killed Maxie?" Max recognized the voice, it was Stitch.

Still rattled his nerves slowly settled down. "Hey man, thanks." Max watched the car's tail-lights brighten and disappear around a corner. "Man, I almost walked right into that car."

Stitch stood Max up straight. He made a perfunctory motion of brushing off Max's coat. When he noticed his cast and the bandage on his nose, his eyes opened wide.

"What happened to you," he said pointing to the cast. "You look like shit. If the other guy looks any worse, I'd say you were in one hell of a fight."

"Thanks, I love you too. I got jumped by four of your cousins."

Stitch looked puzzled. "Cousins?"

"That little bitch friend of yours set four Caucasians on me. She lured me into the alley and they jumped me." Max made a few punching motions. "But I took two out."

He smiled. "Yea laid them out. Probably still there licking their wounds."

Stitch looked him over, turning Max's head side to side inspecting the damage. "How'd they break your nose?" "A big boot. That was an old guy, their leader." Max grimaced as he gently squeezed his nose, which was more swollen now that Addison tweaked it. "They broke my wrist too and hit my forehead with a club." He lifted his cap up to show Stitch the bandage. He was about to run with it, but stopped before any more came out of his mouth. Stitch wasn't stupid and Max didn't want to over-do it.

Stitch gently padded his fingers on the spot. "It doesn't make sense. Addy isn't like that." He stared into Max's eyes, but Max was used to lying and stared back at him in pained innocence. Stitch shook his head. Evidence was Max, his childhood friend, got beaten up. Why, Stitch didn't know, but Max was a friend and as a friend he'd stand by him.

"So what do you want to do? Want me to round up a couple guys? Do you even know who these guys were?"

"Yeah," Max said. "I know where the old man lives and have an idea of where he goes at night. If we grab a couple of guys we could fix him. The others..." Max shrugged his shoulders.

Stitch knew Max and that there had to be more to the story than he was telling. He couldn't in the life of him figure out why Addy would be involved. Maybe Max was mistaken by some set of bad co-incidences. He didn't want to get involved in any of Max's shady plots, but still...

Stitch and Max had been together every day, except when Stitch was in the Marine Corp and served in Iraq.

He also knew the little girl and liked her. Sometimes he'd even leave her a buck or two, when he had it. He admired her tenacity and balls. She didn't take shit from anyone and most importantly she didn't take anyone. She reminded him of the girl he was dating when he was strung out, they had the same ice blue eyes, only his girl had blonde hair. Stitch thought that was a lifetime ago. She had left him all of a sudden, no good bye, no notice. Anyway he knew Addy wouldn't have set Max up, if anything, Max walked into a hornet's nest and got stung.

Max and Stitch, carefully this time, walked across the street. When they got to Max's hideout, Stitch turned and walked home, or what he thought as home, he was crashing on his sister's couch. He hunched his shoulders and plodded down the street wondering what all this drama with Addy was about. He had warned Max a month ago to leave her alone. Max wanted to get Addy to set up old guys, but she wouldn't have anything to do with it. Stitch knew there was no way that she could have set Max up. She cut Max's finger with that little bee stinger she keeps in her pocket, but that was his fault; he tried to take her coat and got too close.

◆ ◆ ◆

Max looked left and then right to see if anyone was watching. Stepping backwards, he just melted into an alley. It was no wider than his skinny frame could squeeze into. Halfway down he leaned over and picked up a section of plywood and jumped into a small recess in the ground, then into his hide-e-hole.

Max smiled, he was home. Home at least until someone found him there and kicked him out, or they knocked down the building for one of those new high rises that seem to be going up everywhere where the rich whiteys live in luxury. Yea! And they pay big money for it too. Now he was living in that same place for free. His only neighbors were a few like him and of course rats and spiders, both of which Max hated. Cockroaches had long since abandoned the building; he figured there was nothing for them to eat after the people left.

Max had no visible income so he couldn't afford to move to a better place. In fact, Max had no income at all and long exhausted his benefits from the state and city. What money he did scrounge up came from snatching up bottles and cans out of garbage cans, maybe every once in a while he would find a drunk passed out in an alley and go through his pockets, but that was seldom.

Max sat in his battered old chair. He dug deep into its cushion and brought out a small vial with tiny white pills, he opened the top and shook out two and smiled. *Every dark cloud has a silver lining.* He popped them into his mouth and swallowed, he didn't have any water so they stuck to his throat, but he managed to finally get them down. He grimaced at the bitter taste they left on his pallet and plotted his revenge. Yea, he smirked. *That little bitch is going to feel pretty damn sorry and so is that old man.* His face broke out into a wide grin.

CHAPTER SIX

THE NEXT EVENING I DECIDED TO GO TO THE PUB at my usual time. It was one of those nights where the wind decided to plague another part of the city and blow somewhere else. I walked at my usual brisk pace with my cane leading the way but not in real use. As I strolled by the alley where I met Addison, I heard an unusual sound coming from inside. I stopped and listened for a minute. In a second's time two sets of hands grabbed me and forcefully shuffled me to the back. By the time I gathered my wits about me I was well inside the alley. I tried to whip my arms about to get away, but they held firm. One of the hooligans let go of my arm with one hand and gave me a sudden and forceful punch to my stomach. I hadn't had time to prepare myself and felt the full force of his strike. The air pushed out of me in a loud grunt and I doubled over. The continued to hustle me along

The light above the pizza parlor door was out and Addison's box was tossed and turned over, however thinking of it now, what difference does it make which side is up. Max stood there with two men at his side, one leaning up against the building partially hidden in darkness. The two men who man-handled me kept a tight grip on my arms with their big beefy paws. I knew what was coming and tried to struggle to free myself, but found I wasn't going anywhere.

"Well, well, well look what the cats dragged in," said Max with a toothy grin, but he looked at me with steady malicious eyes. He had a broom handle in his hand and was slapping on his leg, each time a little harder as his anger swelled. He reminded me of a spider who found a juicy fly stuck to his web. His grin disappeared as he pointed his stick at me, "It's time for you to pay for what you did to me."

I made like I spit at his feet. It was a false sense of bravado I know, but I didn't want to show them I was scared. Most importantly I wanted to show Max my disdain for him.

One of the hoods holding my arm swung his arm back to punch me in the gut. I saw it coming and tightened my stomach muscles. It hurt, but not as much as he wanted. I bent over slightly with a meager grunt. I looked at him defiantly. "My grandmother used to hit harder than that." He gave me a look of disbelief and tightened his grip.

I gave the thug a smirk and tried to raise my cane, but my arm was locked to my side. Actually, I was surprised that the scoundrels allowed me to keep it. I know I would've discarded any weapon, no matter how insignificant.

"Max, I'm surprised you could dig up four friends." I chuckled. "I suppose you're going to beat me up now. Well, get on with it. I've killed better men than you in my life and you can be certain that if nothing else, I will take you down with me."

"Yea?" Max said, "first it's you then I'm gonna get that

little bitch." He slammed the stick on the pavement making a sharp sound that echoed in the alley. He stepped toward me and stopped a foot away. His face twisted into a grimace as he plunged the stick into my gut. I doubled over in pain. The guy leaning up against the building stood slowly. He came out of the darkness and even though he was wearing a hood over his head, I caught a glimpse of his face.

"Max you're not going to do anything to Addison," he said threateningly. "I told you to leave her alone. I told you I what I would do if you bothered her again and I meant it."

Max turned to look at the thug, "Yeah, I know, but she set me up. She deserves what she'll get."

The man who punched me the first time loosened his grip and looked at the hooded thug. He shook his head, "Max, Stitch is right. Leave Addy alone."

In the Marine Corps the first thing we are taught is know your enemy, the second is to divide and conquer. I had an opening.

I straightened up and stretched my stomach muscles. I then yanked my arm loose to free myself and succeeded in getting one arm free. Pushing the other guy off me, I entered the light of the Chinese restaurant. Two sets of hands grabbed me again. Max and the third guy locked eyes, neither one wanted to be the first to turn away. "Did he tell you that I hit him with my cane trying to keep him from raping Addison?" I said.

The hooded guy turned his head toward me. We got a good look at each other. "Gunny?"

A smile broke from my face, "Sgt. Stitcher? What the hell are you doing with this hoodlum?" I demanded. The

Marine in me came out in full force. I struggled to free myself from the two guys holding me and was successful. Both let go, but remained close enough to grab my arms again if necessary.

"Gunny Cramer, you're one of the guys who beat up Max?" His voice showed an edge of incredulousness. He looked Max questionably. Max looked scared.

Max stepped back, "Don't listen to him," he said, panic edging into his voice, "he'll say anything to get out of the beating I'm about to give him." He looked at Stitch and then the others.

"Nonsense," I said, "It was me and me alone who trounced him. You know me, since when do I need anyone else to take out the trash?" I looked from one to the other of the men. "I gave Addison some money and this piece of work here tried to take it from her." Stitch looked at me funny, "I'll explain later." Three of the men looked at Max; one looked at him with exasperation. I could tell he's been through this kind of dilemma before. Max tried to counter my statement, but he fumbled the words. The two guys who held me started to walk out of the alley, but stopped after a few feet. I could tell Stitcher saw the truth of it. He had been a smart Sergeant and a very capable Marine. "I was returning home from the pub, when I heard a commotion in this alley. Max was trying to force her into the back and rape her." My voice was even without a hint of anxiety. "But she put up quite a fight and almost got away."

Max stepped back a few more steps. He looked nervous, like a rat in a cage being lowered into water scrambling and clawing trying to get out.

"Don't believe him, he, he's lying." Max whined and looked at Stitch, "Come on man, you know me. We're bros bro." Max started to edge toward the opening of the alley.

The man who punched me, tall and big shouldered, stepped up to block his way. "I like Addy Max. If you were going to do anything to her I'll shit you myself," he said poking Max in the chest. The menace in his voice struck Max in the face and he started to stammer.

"No man, I didn't," he said as he tried to edge out. But his way was still blocked. He dropped his stick. "Come on guys, he's lying. I didn't do anything to her," he was pleading for his life, "I wasn't going to rape her, I only wanted to scare her. She wouldn't give me any of the money..." He realized he had gone too far.

"Max," said Stitch. "You better find another neighborhood to stay in, this one's off limits to you, as of now." He moved toward Max and got to within a few inches of his face. "I warned you," the menace in his voice rising, "to leave her alone." He grabbed Max by the front of his raincoat. Stitch's hand as large as I ever saw it squeezed the front and brought Max nose to nose. "If I see you tomorrow, I'm going to fuck you up. The only reason I don't do it now is… like you said we were bros." He pushed Max with his powerful hand sending him sprawling.

I giggled a little, it seems Max has a fondness for the alley floor. Soon the only people in the alley were me and SGT. Stitcher. We looked at each other, both thinking of the last time we were together. All the years that separated us disappeared. I smiled at my former sergeant and gave him a hug.

"I haven't seen you in what four, five years?" I said. "I didn't know you lived in New York. What do you say we go have a pint or two?"

Stitcher smiled, "I'd like that Gunny."

As we were leaving the door to Mr. Lim's opened and three young men came out burnishing cleavers. They yelled at us waving their arms in the air. I could only surmise that they were wishing us a pleasant and safe journey. Stitcher and I looked at them and bowed.

We went to the pub and talked about old times and old friends. People we both knew, some gone on to new things and some just gone. Stitcher had been wounded in Iraq and released. He was prescribed pain medication and became addicted to it. He finally got free of it and was trying to get his life together, but it's been hard. When we left the pub, I gave him my card and invited him for Thanksgiving dinner. I owed him that and much, much more. He said he really would like that and to meet Miranda. After an hour and a half of talk we went our separate ways.

I went home and told Miranda of the events in the alley. At first, she showed great concern, but when she heard me mention Sgt. Stitcher and his involvement in aiding Addison, she seemed to calm down. She even agreed that inviting him to our home for Thanksgiving was a good idea and said she hoped he would take my offer to heart.

◆ ◆ ◆

The next night Miranda and I were having a quiet dinner talking over the day's events and the latest news from our daughter, Elizabeth, when the doorbell rang. We looked at each other, both surprised and perplexed. Miranda raised an eyebrow and silently mouthed Addison questioningly. I shrugged and made a face that said I don't know. We don't often get visitors. I arose from the table and went over to the intercom.

"Hello?"

"Mr. Cramer, this is Addison," She sounded hysterical. I could hear the tension and fear in her voice. "Someone cleaned up the alley and all my stuff is gone."

I heard her moaning something unintelligible and looked back at Miranda. I imagined that poor little girl freezing in a cold corner with absolutely nothing for protection.

"Well Richard, don't let her stand out there in the freezing cold, bring her up," Miranda commanded.

Speaking into the microphone I said, "Don't go away, I'll be right down." I turned back to Miranda and she stood up shooing me out the door.

"Quickly, get down there and bring that poor thing up here."

I opened the door and went out. I waited for the elevator. The bell rang and the door slid open. Mrs. Meddleson stood blocking the door clutching her purse in front of her. She gave me quite an angry glare. I burst out laughing. She turned her head and edged as far over to the corner as the wall would allow. I stood bouncing slightly on my toes in front feeling her icy glare. Miranda was going to get a kick out of this. The ride down was silent and strained. One could cut the tension with a knife. I still smiled. Finally the car stopped and the bell dinged as the doors slid open. I strode out first followed closely by the ice maiden. Addison was waiting by the front door, looking every bit as disheveled as ever. Perfect. Opening the door, I felt a rush of cold air. Addison came in and with her an odor beyond belief.

"I'm sorry, but I didn't know what to do," she said trying to keep from crying.

Mrs. Meddleson gagged and gave Addison one look, harrumphed and walked out the door careful not to get too close to Addison.

"Have a good evening Mrs. Meddleson, I hope it's not too cold for you," I said in the most pleasant voiced as I could muster.

She turned around and held up her fore-finger and shook it at me. I shrank back from her icy glare. As least it wasn't the middle finger she shook. I turned toward Addison and laughed. She seemed hurt by my outburst and started for the door.

"I'm sorry. The laugh wasn't for you. That's one of the women in the park the day you were screaming that you didn't want to have sex with me. She went directly to Miranda and told her I was having an affair with a young girl." I took hold of her arm and felt her tense. I let go realizing my mistake, I said, "I'm sorry," and pointed her toward the elevator. "I'm glad you came to us," I said reassuringly.

"I hope I didn't get you in any trouble." Tears welled in her eyes and I could see she had been crying by the trails on her cheeks.

The ride up the elevator was even more strained than the one going down. The cold leached off Addison as did her sour smell. I couldn't help but wince. She looked up at me turning red and lowered her head. She was shivering, but I couldn't tell if it was from the cold or fear being alone with me. I wanted to reassure her that everything would be all right. I didn't want to touch her in any way for fear she would start screaming, like she did in the park. I cast side glances at her, while she stared at the floor. Just before we reached my floor, I couldn't help myself and gave her a small reassuring hug. It was more like a shoulder squeeze. She tensed again and glared at me for a second.

I took my hand away. "Don't worry, you'll be safe here," I said in a soothing voice. She continued to cry. She was shaking slightly more now and I knew she was thinking she made a mistake in coming here.

The elevator stopped and the bell dinged just before the doors opened. Addison looked up and stared out at the wall on the opposite side of the hall. I began to go out and stopping in the door I turned to her and held out my hand, palm up. She looked at me, but didn't move.

"I promise you," I said, "if at any time you wish to leave, we won't stop you." I gave her a small smile. "It's up to you, you have the power to go or stay."

She made a tiny gesture to move forward but stopped. I could see this was a huge step for her, she didn't want to relinquish her freedom or her tenuous control of her life. She looked at me and then past me. The door tried to close with another ding but was stopped by my body and as it opened again the bell dinged again.

Addison's eyes changed from fear to relief. I felt a presence behind me and could smell a slight scent of Chanel.

I turned and there was Miranda.

"Well," she said annoyed staring at me, "are you going to invite Addison in or are you two going to stand here all night listening to the door chime." She looked at Addison. "Come Addison let's get you into some place warm," Miranda said in a motherly voice.

"Actually, I thought we would wait here until Mrs. Meddleson came home," I retorted.

Miranda looked at me perplexed. She held her hand out to Addison, "Come, join us. You're welcome in our home." She held out her arm ushering her off the elevator and pointing the way to our home.

Miranda directed Addison to sit down at the dining table. She lowered herself into the chair not taking her coat off. Miranda sat next to her and I sat in the opposite. During all this, Miranda didn't even once make a face or show displeasure in the way Addison smelled.

"Tell us what happened," Miranda said.

"I got delayed coming home, when I got back to the alley; it was clean. Everything." Addison hung her head in her hands and trembled. Tears leaked out from her fingers as she tried to get control of her emotions. "My blanket and tarp were the only things I had. Now they're gone."

"When was the last time you were in the alley?" I asked. This seemed like an awful sudden turn of events. One doesn't just clean an alley on the spur of the minute.

"This morning," she said looking at me. "It was just starting to get light out. I hid my tarp, I usually wrap my blanket around me under my coat, but it seemed warmer, so I hid it with the tarp."

"Was there any indication that it was going to be cleaned? Did anyone say anything at all?" Miranda asked as she put her hand on Addison's. Addison's first reaction was to jerk her hand away, but she left it and shook her head slowly.

"I didn't have a lot, but it was mine." This she said with such determination, that it lent me to believe that she valued her possessions. "Why did they throw everything away? I wasn't taking up much room. I kept my area as clean as I could keep it. I didn't... I made sure I used public restrooms when I could." She looked at us, fright written all over her face. "What am I going to do?"

Miranda, in a motherly way, cupped her hand under Addison's chin. She felt the tension in her jaw and withdrew her hand with a hint of a smile that suggested she knew the answer. Addison looked at Miranda with sad trusting eyes and relinquished her independence.

"First, you're going to have something hot to eat." Her tone left no room for debate. "Then you can have a hot bath or a shower if you prefer. After which, we'll show you to your room for the night. I have some pajamas that may somewhat fit you, if you tie them tight." Addison looked down in embarrassment. "I'll wash and dry your clothes so you'll have something clean to wear tomorrow."

Addison raised her eyes to meet Miranda's. The constant strain of the last six months caused Addison to be taut, like an overly tight rope being twisted to the point of snapping all together. She felt it ease just a little, to loosen on her body and for the first time she knew she could let down her guard, just a little.

"Tomorrow," Continued Miranda, "we'll talk about your options. Gunny and I will come up with several plans of action," She cupped her hand to her mouth whispering, "He was a Marine you know." She winked at him, "He's used to coming up with plans of action. O.K.?" She rose from the chair. "Right now you need something hot to eat and a good night's sleep in a warm friendly bed." She squeezed Addison's shoulder, "Everything will look a little better in the morning." Addison nodded. "Let me have this coat and I'll put it... somewhere for you."

Addison stood and slipped off the socks on her hands and stuffed them into the pockets then unbuttoned the three remaining buttons and untied the two strings that held it tight to her body. She slowly, reluctantly took of the one thing that protected her from the weather and the leers of men who were in the same dilemma as she. Addison handed over the coat reluctantly. She took off her hat and handed it to Miranda. Unzipping her hoodie she gave that up last. Both Richard and Miranda gawked at her emaciated state. Her wrists that stuck out from the ends of her shirt were just bones. They could tell she was close to starving. Addison's baggy pants looked empty and now on closer inspection they saw how hallowed her cheeks were. Miranda wondered why this young woman wasn't in a hospital.

Miranda fingered them as if something was lurking inside ready to bite her and stuffed it into a large garbage bag.

"We'll think of what to do with those tomorrow." She brought the bag over to the balcony door and put it outside.

"Now sit," she said putting a hand on Addison's shoulder. "I hope you like tomato bisque."

Addison gazed up at Miranda and gave a timid little nod and then she watched Miranda hurry into the kitchen. Addison sat at the dining table all scrunched up, as if trying to disappear. *I shouldn't be here. Maybe I should get up and leave. Richard said I could leave at any time. But where can I go?* She kept her head tilted down staring at her lap watching her hands twist relentlessly under the table. She tried not to move, to make a stir, anything which would bring attention to her. She felt Richard's eyes glued to her, but she didn't want to meet them. The noises of food being prepared floated from the kitchen. Soon a hint of tomato wafted and Addison's stomach gurgled. *What's a bisque?* She felt her face grow hot and prickly.

"Smells good," Richard murmured. "Miranda is an excellent cook." Addison lifted her head and peeked at him. "She is very good at everything she does, especially when it comes to making soup."

Richard thought that Addison shrank just a little. He went back to just observing her. She continued to have constant movements with her hands and her gaze returned to her lap.

She is so afraid. What made her so afraid that she can't relax? I wonder if it's me or men in general. No, she just isn't comfortable here in a strange environment with two people she doesn't know. She didn't act this way in the park. He sat in silence. The noises in the kitchen had abated. *She was in her element. That's why she felt more comfortable.*

Occasionally Addison peeked at Richard and when

he turned to her, she quickly looked away. Richard had a strange smile on his face. One that Addison had seen often, one she recognized as pity. She didn't want anyone's pity and she prickled. She stopped fidgeting with her hands and glared at Richard.

"Don't pity me," she said quietly. "I don't want anyone's pity."

"I'm sorry," he replied. "I don't pity you. I feel sad, that's all. Sad that for some reason you have found yourself in this position. But pity, no. I think you have done quite well for someone your age to stay alive and not become like that guy who attacked you."

The conversation ended there. Addison looked around the room. She saw photos of a girl at different stages of her life. Then she noticed pictures of a small child with an older version of the little girl. Her head slowly turned and studied everything, knickknacks, paintings, furniture. It all looked clean, not new, not warn, well taken care of.

Her head stopped at a photograph of a young man and woman. The woman dressed in a nice dress with a bouquet and a large smile that extended to shining eyes. The man dressed in a blue uniform holding a white hat. His hair, cut so short you could see the sun shining off bare skin, he also was beaming. Addison studied that photo and looked at Richard.

"That was taken," Richard said, "on our wedding day, forty years ago." His mind ventured to the past. "I had just received my orders to Viet Nam, my second tour. I met Miranda while serving as a recruiter in the city. She and I dated and fell in love. The day I got orders I asked her to marry me." His eyes shined with treasured memories. "We were married three days later."

Addison stared at Richard. *I hope I find someone who will love me for forty years.* Her gazed turned to the pictures of the girl.

"Is that of your daughter?" She asked pointing to the photos.

"Yes," Richard replied. "Elizabeth and that's her daughter, Nancy." A smile crossed his face. "She's cutest little girl on the face of the Earth."

We sat in silence; I continued to study Addison imagining what could have led her here. She occasionally looked up at me and smiled nervously. I can't help but feel an overwhelming sense of respect for her boldness and courage to live out in the street and still renounce the stigma that goes with that lifestyle. It made me wonder how many other people are like her. I knew little about her, but had a great sense of her make-up. I wanted to know more, I wanted to know everything about her. I'm not saying she became my cause. Only that I wanted to help her, not out of the boredom in my life, but in helping her I realized that there are other things I can do than feed squirrels in the park. I need something that will make a difference. It's time that I get off my retired ass and do something worthwhile, something to make this city a better place.

Miranda came into the room with a flourish and placed a large bowl of tomato bisque in front of Addison and went back into the kitchen. Steam floated up out of the bowl and into her face. She breathed in the aroma, rich and sweet with an earthly quality. She tentatively took the spoon and dipped it into the bowl. Her nervousness in the company of strangers showed in her shaking hand and soup spilled off the outer edges of the spoon. She sipped what was left. The bisque was hot and made her lips pucker as she put it in her mouth. She blew on the next spoonful for a couple of seconds and again put it to her lips. The silky liquid slid smoothly down her throat and her eyes lit up and she smiled.

"Um," she said with closed eyes. "This is good." And when Miranda returned she asked, "Did you make this?"

"Yes, I'm the chief cook and bottle washer in this outfit. Richard helps out, but not with cooking." Miranda held a plate of grilled chicken with corn and brown rice. She set it down next to the soup. A moment later she had a cup of hot chocolate in her hand and placed it next to the plate.

We learned that she hadn't eaten like this in months and it showed by the hurried way she devoured the soup and chicken. The charities and soup kitchens were often full and she found that many of the volunteers stared at her and whispered to each other as they nodded toward her. She didn't want to be taken into custody, so she stayed away from them. The hot chocolate was too much for her. It brought back memories of happier times with the family she lived with after her mother died. They used to drink hot chocolate by the fireplace on cold winter nights. Looking down into the rich brown liquid, she silently mourned and tears began to fall.

Miranda noticed she hadn't touched the drink. Addison sat staring. A tear splashed into the cup, spreading the foam. Miranda reached out to Addison's hand and gave a gentle squeeze.

"Honey, what's the matter."

Addison turned toward Miranda, tears rolling down her face cleansing grime. "Why are you being nice to me? What do I have to do…?"

Miranda moved her chair close to Addison and put her arm around her shoulder. She felt Addison tense, but held on. Slowly her muscles relaxed. "You don't have to do anything." She wiped the tears from Addison's face with her fingers. "Just be you."

Miranda looked at Richard. With a knuckle she swiped an eye. She took Addison's hand. "Come, I think a hot shower and a good night's sleep will do you good." She looked into Addison's eyes and wiped the new tears away and then kissed her on the forehead. "Come on, let's get you out of those dirty clothes. I'll give you a pair of P.J.s, O.K.?" Addison nodded and weakly smiled.

◆ ◆ ◆

Addison stayed in the shower for a long time. She let the water flow all over her and breathed in the hot steam. It had a medicinal effect on her and she started to feel just a little better. At the shelters the water wasn't all together hot and they gave you a three minute time limit. When finished she wiped the mirror clear of moisture with a towel and looked at her image. She didn't like the looks of the skinny girl with hallowed cheeks and dark rings around her eyes staring back at her.

After the shower Miranda showed Addison to a bedroom and gave her a hug good night. Addison held on for a long time not wanting to let go. She hadn't felt a human touch in six months. She needed to savor every second, for she didn't know if there would any more.

Miranda gasped and felt a slight sting in her eyes. She rubbed Addison's back in slow reassuring circles, then leaned over and kissed the top of her head. Miranda breathed in deeply and let go. It has been a long time since she felt the young body of her daughter.

"Get a good night's sleep," she said heavily and exited the room, gently closing the door.

Addison walked around the room looking at all the mementos of the girl that once slept here. She looked at the bed and drew the covers down. She pushed on the mattress to test for softness and ran her hand over the clean powder blue sheets and bent to smell them. Smiling, she thought they smelled like Gain. She shut off the light, got into bed and pulled the covers up to her chin. Staring at the black ceiling, tears streamed down the sides of her face. *What am I going to do?* It didn't take long for her to fall soundly and fitfully asleep.

❖ ❖ ❖

"Thank you," murmured Richard while Miranda washed the dishes. "I'll dry."

"She's so frail." Miranda peeked over her shoulder at the man she'd been married to for forty years. "She won't last the winter. I know, I've seen them come into the hospital on their last legs. They catch a cold and soon it turns into something else. Their systems are weakened by mal-nutrition. Some we could save; others…"

"We have to save this one," Richard said determinedly. "Addison is special, I can feel it."

Richard picked up a towel and began to dry dishes. Miranda stared at him in disbelief a tear rolled down his cheek. A smile crept across her face.

Miranda looked in on Addison just before going to bed. Addison was sound asleep with her head sticking out of the covers and the sound she made reminded Miranda of a cat purring.

CHAPTER SEVEN

THE NEXT MORNING RICHARD AND MIRANDA were having coffee at the dining table. Speaking in hushed voices, they didn't want to wake Addison or let her know what they were discussing.

"She is all skin and bones," Miranda said incredulously. "I can't imagine how she survived this long with the diet she's been eating." She grabbed Richard's hand squeezing it hard. Her nails dug into his skin, but he didn't budge. "You saw her eating out of a garbage can. Luckily she doesn't have any vermin on her. I examined her, all over."

Miranda smiled at the shock on Addison's face when she started to squeeze, probe and prod her body.

"At first she balked, but when I told I had been a nurse for forty years, she co-operated. She was able to take a shower once a week, but not steadily, at one of the shelters, but she didn't like the looks men gave her and she left quickly. Still it'll take a week of hot showers and a good stiff brush to get the grime out of her finger nails."

"Oh," Richard said, "are we going to let her stay for a week?" Inwardly he smiled. He missed having his daughter and granddaughter home for the holidays. He enjoyed the sound of the pattering feet and the squabbling of between a mother and daughter. He did enjoy the comfort of Miranda's company and her sole attention, but he found the laughter of children a relief from the duties of Marine life.

"Well," she said with a hint of irritation, "would you have me throw her back out into the street?" When she noticed the twinkle in his eyes she playfully slapped his arm. "Richard, sometimes you can be irritating," She said a little testily.

"She found that alley only a month ago. I don't know where she had been before that, but I can imagine." Richard saw that Miranda shuttered. "The proprietor of the Chinese restaurant tried to chase her away, yelling at her and threatening to call the police and once even raised a meat cleaver at her." With a tinge of anger she continued. "I'm willing to bet that it was he that orchestrated the clean-up." Richard listened to Miranda. "Luckily she isn't ridden with lice and fleas." She was starting to repeat herself which showed Richard she was becoming angry. "I guarantee if she stays out on the street much longer she won't remain that way." Miranda got up and poured more coffee into their cups. "The longer she stays out there the chance she will die grows enormously. Lord knows what dangers she's had to avoid already." She gave Richard a cold stare, "Are you listening to me Richard?" He nodded trying hard to keep a concerned look on his face. "There must be something we can do for her?" Richard knew what was coming. Miranda rose up and went over to the coffee pot and brought it back to the table to pour more coffee. She realized she had already poured the cups to the rims. Richard smiled at her expression, she glared at him and he quickly rubbed the smile from his face. She sat down heavily. "Richard, we have to take care of her. There seems to be no one else, so it must fall onto our laps." Miranda nodded once. It was final. *Addison will come to live with us. I hope she agrees or there will be no dealing with Miranda for a while.* Richard pretended to yawn to cover his smile, it was an extended yawn, which Miranda knew was fake and she smiled too.

"What if she doesn't want to live with us?" He asked innocently. "What if she prefers to remain out on the street?"

"Non-sense, what young girl in her right mind and Addison is in her right mind, would wish to remain out there," She said incredulously. "I swear Richard; sometimes you say the dumbest things." She took a deep breath. "If we can't convince her to stay with us, then we will convince her to seek assistance." Her expression conveyed that her mind was made up and there would be no back-tracking. Richard knew better than to try to change Miranda's mind once it was set. "She can't last much longer on the street. She's too young to be on her own. What if she falls into the wrong hands, like that hoodlum? I won't let that happen, I just won't."

They heard the door to the bedroom open and both turned toward the sound of shuffling feet sliding down the hall to the bathroom and then that door close. Richard and Miranda looked at each other apprehensively. He took her hand in his and rubbed her fingers. He was proud of his wife, she always knew the right thing to do and wasn't afraid to do it.

"You're right," he said, "we'll talk to her." He raised her hand and kissed her fingers.

A moment later the bathroom door opened. They heard the swishing of Addison's bare feet and bathrobe come down the hall. She came into the dining room eyes sunken and hair in a tussle. She scratched her head with both hands.

"Thank you for letting me stay here last night. I didn't know where to go. I don't like shelters, many of the people are covered with bugs and they give me strange looks. I thought if I stayed out of them I might not get bugs." She yawned, "I didn't realize how much I missed sleeping in a bed where it was warm and secure." She stretched out her arms and twisted her back extending the muscles. "I usually wake at the slightest noise. I don't think I've slept this soundly through the night since I've been out on the street."

"Addison sit down and join us for breakfast," Richard pointed to a chair. "Would you like some bacon and eggs?"

Addison scratched her head again. She wrapped the robe tightly around her, smiling at warmth.

"Yes please, if it's not too much…"

"You're our guest and it's no trouble at all," said Miranda and she went into the kitchen.

Addison looked around the room studying all the knick-knacks of a forty year marriage. She stopped at the photo of the young women smiling with her arms around a little girl. Her face twisted in pain and a tear trickled down an eye.

"She's lucky," Addison said pointing to the photo on the mantle.

Richard looked at her curiously, "Why?"

"They're together."

Richard realized that the picture of his daughter with her child set off memories of Addison's past. He wanted to pursue the matter, but decided to wait until Miranda could listen. He got up and went over to the coffee pot. "Do you drink coffee?" And as he poured her some he continued, "Elizabeth and Nancy live out of state, in Oregon."

Addison sipped the hot brew, it had the right amount of earthiness and wasn't too bitter. Most of all it was fresh, not stale tasting like it had been sitting on the heat for hours. She scratched her head vigorously again.

Miranda came in and set the table. "You have a bad case of dandruff," she squeezed her shoulder, "probably from wearing the knit hat all the time." She didn't stress her unwashed hair. "I can give you some medicated shampoo, if you like. It will clear it up in less than a week."

Addison turned red and looked down at the table. She nodded. "Please." She raised her eyes up to Miranda, "What about my clothes?"

"I've washed them and tried to sew them," Miranda grimaced thinking of the grime and smell, "but they're in bad shape. We can get you new clothes, if you like. Your pants had large rips in them. I'm really surprised they gave you any comfort from the cold. Your shirt was way too big for you." Miranda went to the closet and pulled out a bag. She showed Addison the rips and shirt tag. "You only have these summer shoes, you can keep them, but you really need a pair of winter shoes. If you like we can buy a pair for you.

Addison breathed in deeply, "I guessed I've really mucked things up for myself. I had some other clothes, but they were thrown away with everything else."

"No," Richard interjected, "we think you've done quite well for someone so young. How old are you?"

"Fourteen," she whispered. She looked down face blushing.

Richard and Miranda gawked at each other. "Fourteen," they uttered in unison.

"And living on your own for what six months?" Addison nodded. "I think," Miranda said, "you did better than most could. You didn't succumb to drugs or alcohol, that I'm pretty sure." After forty years as a nurse, she developed an exceptional knowledge of the signs of drug and alcohol problems. "You look starved, but that can be taken cared of quickly. We're both amazed."

Miranda's arm slid around Addison. Addison felt its warmth and relaxed. She remembered her first fostermother doing the same thing. She remembered Mrs. Jenkins holding her like this and the feeling of all the horrors of the world disappearing. Addison melted into that arm's embrace. The feeling of relief and love swept over her and she wanted to embrace it for as long as it would last.

Miranda drew Addison close, she turned and kissed the top of her head, "We have something to talk to you about, but not now." She sprung up, "Now, I think you should have something to eat." She smiled down at her charge. "Would you like some of the bacon and eggs Richard mentioned?"

Addison seemed hesitant, "Go ahead have some," said Richard. "She loves cooking and besides, I would like some bacon and eggs and maybe a pancake or two."

Miranda raised an eyebrow at Richard. He smirked in return. "And what about your cholesterol?"

"One morning of blueberry pancakes won't make much of a difference," he said benignly. "Will it?"

"All right, one egg and one pancake," Miranda acquiesced. "How about you Addison?"

Addison face turned into a big smile, "Yes please, and thank you."

Addison attacked her meal and after finishing breakfast Miranda said, "I have a pair of old sweats that you could wear, if we tied them tight. We'll get dressed and then walk over to Target and pick up some clothes for you and a pair of winter shoes. O.K.?"

♦ ♦ ♦

They returned three hours later with two big bags of clothing. Addison hadn't felt so human in many, many months. Sharing this experience with Miranda, a mother figure was all she could hope for. They commiserated on what to buy, color, usefulness. They had a bite to eat in the food court of the shopping center. They quietly ate their meals, neither feeling comfortable enough to ask questions or to answer them.

Richard smiled as they entered the door. Miranda loved to shop, he often thought she could've made a good living shopping for other women who were too busy to do it themselves. Often when she shopped she would drag him from store to store browsing and buying. He knew he was there just to hold the bags, but he bared it, for he loved her and would do anything she wanted him to do.

Addison put all the bags in the room where she slept. She walked out heavily, as if in a dream. Miranda sat on the sofa and Richard in his chair, elbows on his knees, waiting. She sat down in the middle of the sofa.

"I don't know why you are being so nice to me." Addison said looking down at her hands. "I don't know how I can ever pay you back."

Miranda turned to Addison. "Non-sense, you don't have to repay us," she said. She turned her head to Richard raising her eyebrows. "You need help and we want to give you that help. Right Richard?"

He nodded, "Yes," he said emphatically, "that's correct. In fact, Miranda and I were talking this morning before you joined us. We'd like to have you stay with us, if that's all right with you." He turned to Miranda for assurance.

Miranda nodded and smiled, "Would you like that? I know you don't know us, but I'm sure we could work things out." She noted Addison's confused expression. "Look, you don't have to say yea or nay right now. Think about it. At least stay until after Thanksgiving."

Addison's heart began to pump fast and hard. She churned her hands until her fingers got all tangled. She pounded her hands into her lap.

Richard sat down beside her and cupped his hands over hers. She did not jerk hers away or tense up. He smiled. *I think we're making progress.* "Addison," he said softly, "I know you value your independence. I feel you would like to say yes, but somewhere there's a little voice saying we will turn you into us." He looked into her eyes and smiled. "Am I right?"

"You don't even know me." Addison said. She twisted her head, "How do you know I won't steal you blind?" She looked from one to the other. "I screamed at you and called you a pervert."

"Technically, you didn't." Richard replied with a smile. "You may have implied it, but you actually didn't say it."

"You're correct, we don't really know you, but we know a lot about you. More than you'd expect." Miranda put her arm around Addison's shoulder. She bent forward and looked straight into her eyes. "Just because I didn't meet you until the other day, doesn't mean I don't know who you are. Your demeanor states volumes about you. You don't take from people, like when Richard kept offering you money. You still have a sense of humanity in caring for those cats in the alley and feeding squirrels in the park. You're not on drugs and you kept yourself clean, to a degree. And you only came here in desperation. That suggests to us you are very independent, that's a very good quality and you are a fighter." She squeezed Addison's shoulder. "So you see we know quite a bit about you."

CHAPTER EIGHT

ADDISON HAD ALL THE HOPE IN THE WORLD. She would like to stay with these nice people, but she was broken with memories and agonies of a past life. No one wanted her as she is now, no one wants a fourteen year old girl that likes to dress the way she does, in black, mourning for a family taken from her. Everyone wants her to change. This couple is like the image of grandparents she often wished she had. But like all adults, they would want her to be a younger version of themselves.

Tired of living on the street and constantly of being on her guard, mistrusting everyone, Addison wants to have a stable life like other girls her age. She sees them across the street, laughing, giggling hunched over telling each other secrets, probably about boys or they'd walk right by her but wouldn't see her, unless they got too close to her and then they'd hurry away. Sometimes it made her feel like a ghost. She wants to go to school and get an education that will make her a successful adult. Her longing to have friends, go to parties and maybe when a little older go out on a date, makes her want to succumb to the demands of foster parents. These are some of the things Addison wished she could have. Sometimes at night inside her box or under the quilt in a different alley she dreamt of being well-liked. She dreamt of finding her sister Izzy. They haven't seen each other since they were torn from each other, that was over eleven years ago. That was the one thing she longed for most of all. She would give everything else up to achieve that. All the other stuff was fluff to her, something to think about, something to wish for, but not really necessary in life.

But her independence keeps getting in the way.

"I appreciate your offer, I really do." Addison's closed her eyes and breathed in deeply. When she opened them a tear clung her lashes. "But, I couldn't be who I want to be."

Richard's knitted eyebrows showed confusion. "And who do you want to be?" He said.

"Me! I want to dress the way I like, have my ears pierced, if I choose and to listen to the music I like, hang around friends of my choosing." Addison shook her head, "I don't know." She said showing her frustration. "The last family I was with wanted me to dress like them and read the bible for an hour every night after supper. They wouldn't let me have the friends I wanted, they were always dictating what was good for me. It was so confining, I ran away." She looked from Miranda to Richard and back. "I know it must seem silly to you, but they wouldn't let me be me. I don't think I'm a bad person. I surely know right from wrong and what's good for me and to stay away from what's not." Quickly she added. "Don't get me wrong, they weren't bad people. I even like them and their daughter Megan, but they said I was a bad influence on her as I am and wanted me to change. So I ran away."

"Do you think you could have handled that differently?"

Richard asked. He glanced at Miranda who sat there pondering how they should proceed.

Addison looked contrite. "At the time I really couldn't think of any."

"Have you contacted them since you left?" Miranda asked. "Just to let them know you are all right."

Looking down, Addison slowly shook her head. "I really am sorry if I hurt them." She looked at Miranda. "But if I staid, I think I would've caused a lot of trouble and they would end up hating me. I didn't want that."

Richard enfolded her hand in his. "There are always solutions. Sometimes they may not be what we exactly hope to achieve and will require some concessions by both parties. If we sit down and have a reasonable conversation, we can always come up with a compromise."

Miranda positioned herself on the sofa to look directly into Addison's eyes, there would be no misunderstanding in what she had to say. She rubbed Addison's upper arm. Addison felt its warmth and also its firmness.

"I will be plain, so there is no misunderstanding." Her voice was firm but had a tone of understanding. "If you stay with us there will be rules. We all have to follow some type of rules. You can be whoever you want to be, that is with parameters." Miranda's tone was both firm and loving. "No drugs, no cigarettes, no boys in the apartment when one of us is not present. You must go to school and get good grades. Maybe, when you are sixteen you'll be able to get a job, of which, you will put half in a savings account, the rest will be yours to do what you will. Other than that you can be who you want to be." Miranda raised an eyebrow,

"Do we have a contract?"

It didn't take Addison to make up her mind. She smiled. Seconds passed and the smile faded and a look of confusion settled on her face. "Why are you doing this for me?"

"Because, we believe you need someone to help you." Richard squeezed Addison's hand. "What do you say?" He extended his hand to her. "Do we have a deal?"

Addison lifted her head. She took his hand and nodded, "We do."

Miranda got to her feet and said ebulliently, "Well, now that that's resolved, who wants some hot chocolate?" She stepped into the kitchen with Addison in tow.

Once in the kitchen, Addison crept up beside Miranda. She hung her head down and remained silent. Miranda gazed at her. Addison's lip was trembling and Miranda put her arm around her. Addison reciprocated. "Thank you," she murmured. Miranda turned to her and gave her a big hug. Addison felt sure she made the right decision. She knew Richard was right, any disagreements that arise would have to be hashed out and a compromise agreed upon. She suddenly she felt safe and maybe someday she'll even feel loved.

Miranda stroked the back of Addison's head. *I'll take care of you as I did my daughter. You won't be broken anymore.* She felt a moist warm spot on her shirt growing.

"Come help me with the hot chocolate," Miranda whispered after a minute. They broke away and fixed three cups. Richard was sitting at the dining table when the two women entered with steaming hot liquid and mounds of creamy white foam on top. Miranda set one down in front of Richard and moved to an opposite chair.

Addison sat between them. She stared down into the cup and felt the steamy warmth. She breathed in the smell of chocolate, sweet and earthy. She closed her eyes and let the aroma take her back to a happier time when she lived with the first foster family.

"Now that we are all going to live together," said Miranda, "I think it is time you tell us how you ended up on the street." She reached over and squeezed Addison's hand.

"My father passed away when I was a baby," Addison stared at the cup of brown liquid, like she was concentrating on the past, "I never knew him." Richard and Miranda eyed each other. "My mother died when I was three." Her eyes began to glaze over. "I only remember bits and pieces of that time. I don't have any pictures of her or my sister, Izzy. We had no relatives so we were separated and given to different foster families. I never found out where my sister ended up. I went with the Simpsons and stayed with them until I was ten." Addison remained silent for a few minutes. Her fingers rubbed against each other as she remembered the last few days with that family.

"Honey," said Miranda with great concern. She knew Addison was struggling to both remember and come to terms with something that plagued her for many years. Miranda had seen the same expression many times over the years in the eyes of trauma victims. "Take all the time you need and continue when you're ready."

Addison rubbed her hands on her pants, as if trying to erase a stigma that has haunted her.

"I, at the time, didn't realize what was happening."

Her breathing elevated. "Ever since I join the family, Tom, Carol's husband, would play bouncy with me and their two girls. We would get up on his knee and he would bounce us up and down," A sad smile appeared, "we would giggle and laugh, all three of us. Sandy and Linda were two and three years older than me. When they became too big to sit on Tom's knee, it would only be me to play bouncy. Soon I got too big." Tears seeped out of the corners of her eyes and one dropped into the cooling liquid making a tiny splash. "One day we were talking about when we kids were little and the fun we used to have. Linda mentioned bouncy and how she missed it. Sandy and Carol were in the kitchen preparing supper and Linda went into her room. Tom asked me if I wanted to play bouncy."

Miranda and Richard looked at each other. Their faces were grim. Both knew where the story was leading. Addison's face streamed with tears. Her voice broke.

"I wanted to relive that memory, when we did it... it... it felt like I belonged and I wasn't an intruder. I climbed on his lap and he started to bounce me.... Only it wasn't like it used to be, it was somehow different. Within a minute I slid off his knees and into his lap. After a minute, I turned to see if he was getting tired. He looked like he was going to sneeze, but he didn't. Soon he stopped. He pushed me off his lap, got up and quickly went into their bedroom."

"At supper, he didn't say anything and wouldn't look at me. I felt that I must have done something wrong, but I didn't know what and I was afraid to ask Carol, for she might get mad at me too. All that night I looked at Tom, but he would just pretend I wasn't there. Carol sensed something was different and she kept watching the two of us." Addison looked up at Miranda, but not Richard. She saw the same look in Miranda's eyes as she remembered were in Carol's. Fright filled Addison's heart, did she say too much?

Miranda got up, sat in the chair next to Addison and put her arm around her. She drew her to her bosom stroking her head gently. "Addison, you didn't do anything wrong, you were but a child," she said in a motherly way. "What he," She emphasized 'he' with loathing, "did was despicable. She looked at Richard with a worried look. "How long did this continue?"

"The next day Carol brought the two girls to band practice. I was home finishing homework. Tom came home early from work. He asked me if I needed help with my homework. I said no. He stood in the doorway to my room. I felt happy, he wasn't mad at me anymore. He said he really enjoyed playing bouncy with me. I looked at him and said I did too. He looked pale, like he was sick. Then he asked if I wanted to play bouncy again, but he sounded so strange." Silence prevailed in the room for what seemed like minutes. "I don't know why I said yes, I felt something was different, wrong, but I didn't want Tom to be mad at me again, so I got on his lap and he placed his hands in my lap. This time when we were playing he stopped and said he would like to try it with me facing him."

Richard squeezed his hand into a tight fist under the table. Miranda reached over to calm him. He gave her a look of helpless outrage.

"We did it both ways when the three of us were young,

so I didn't think it all that bad. Only now, after we continued, he became out of breath just like I do when I run hard for a long time.

"We didn't know the front door opened. Nor did we hear Carol or the girls come in. They were standing in the doorway when Tom groaned." Addison put her head in her hands and cried. Miranda comforted her. It took fifteen minutes for her to regain her composure.

"Honey," Miranda said with the softest voice. "I think that is enough for today. Maybe you should lie down and take a nap."

Addison looked up at both of them with red rimmed eyes and mucus running down from her nose. "No, I need to tell you this." She rubbed her eyes with her sleeve. "I need to say it out loud, I never talked about it to anybody."

Miranda scurried into the kitchen and returned with a clean dishtowel wet with cool water and washed Addison's face. "Why don't we continue this later?"

"Please let me finish?" She pleaded. She looked from one to the other, both nodded once. It was a reluctant approval.

"Carol started screaming at me, then at Tom. The two girls stood in the doorway frozen, confused shaking their heads. Carol told Tom to get out as she entered my room and started opening my drawers. When Tom left, I saw he had a big wet spot on his pants and I started to giggle that Carol scared him so bad that he peed his pants. It was years later that I realized what I had done."

"No honey, you didn't do anything wrong. It was

Tom's fault. Don't ever think that you caused this, you were too young."

"That's right," Richard put in, "you're not the one to blame for what happened."

Addison looked at Richard with a blank look and nodded. "That afternoon Carol took me to child welfare and left me there. She didn't say a word nor even look at me. She just brought me into the office, talked to my case worker and left."

"That night I was put into an emergency home and from there I went from home to home. That lasted for three years." Addison wrung her hands again. She hugged herself and rocked. "It seemed nobody wanted me. I felt tainted. It had to be me if no one wanted me, right?" She scanned the two faces. "I was the common denominator. Four families discarded me. Four families felt I was unfixable."

Miranda rubbed Addison's back, "We won't discard you honey." She glanced at Richard.

"Most definitely not and you are not tainted." Richard cupped his hand on Addison's chin and peered into her eyes. "If you give us a chance, we'll work it out." A sad smile grew.

Addison sniffed and nodded.

Who were the last people you were with?" Miranda asked.

"That was the Andersons. They took me in, but wanted me to be exactly like them. I tried to, I really did. But it became too confining there. They dictated everything I could do, just like their children. I was with them for six months, before I ran away."

Addison took a deep breath. She had never told any of this to anyone before. Somehow it felt good. It was a relief to get it off her chest and out in the open for all to see. She felt like a deflated balloon, one that had expelled all the bad air, poisoned air.

"You mentioned a sister," said Miranda, "where is she right now?"

"Yes, her name is Izzy. At least that is what I remember it to be. I don't know where she is."

"Why weren't you put in the same house?" Miranda continued.

Addison shook her head. Richard snorted his disapproval. Miranda glanced at him giving a sign to say nothing.

"I tried to find her on the internet, but had no luck. Social Services couldn't help. They said they tried to find her, but said there was no one in their files with her name." Addison stared at Miranda with a determined expression. "I'll find her someday, I will. Everywhere I go, I look for someone who looks like me, someone with black hair and blue eyes. Sometimes I find a woman like that and I go up to her and call 'Izzy', but they just walk away thinking I'm demented, get mad or hand me a little change."

Miranda lifted her cup of cocoa and took a sip. It was cold and she winced.

"My drink is cold, does anyone want a fresh cup?" She looked from Richard to Addison. Both nodded yes. She rose from her chair and started for the kitchen, "Do you want to help me Addison?"

"Yes please. It will help me to get my mind off what I just told you." She grabbed Richard's cup and followed Miranda.

When they sat back down at the dining table Miranda sipped her drink, "Oh, that's much better. We could help you look for your sister, if you want." She held up her hand to Addison stemming off any response. "I'm not promising anything, but we could try. We have a friend in the building who works for child placement in CPS. Right Richard?" Richard nodded. "Yes, we'll talk to her this evening." He looked at his watch. "In fact, we could call her right now." He noticed Addison didn't seem happy. "What's wrong? Don't you want our help?"

"Yes, I really do. If I could find my sister everything would be all right, but she can't be found." She looked down into her hot chocolate, "and CPS will take me away."

"Oh… Well…" Miranda looked thoughtfully. "Barbara is a friend of ours." Miranda thought quickly hoping she wasn't misleading Addison. "I'm sure if we ask her she will help us on the Q.T. She's known us for many years and knows we don't have a lifestyle that would jeopardize a young woman's well-being. I'm sure we could talk her into helping us, and then if nothing comes of it, she can help us keep you here, if you like."

"Well… if you… think so." Addison said with uncertainty. But she was willing to trust in their judgement. "I just don't want to be put in another foster home."

Miranda got up to make more hot chocolate. While she was waiting for the water to get hot in the tea kettle Addison walked up to her and stood beside her.

"Thank you for everything you and Richard are doing for me." Addison put her arms around Miranda and squeeze tightly.

Miranda thought, it was as if Addison was trying to hold onto life. She returned her hug and kissed her on the top of her head. "You're welcome," she said. Steam began to shoot out of the tea kettle in an ear-piercing squeal, but it not bring that tender moment to an end.

◆ ◆ ◆

That evening after supper there was a knock on the door. Richard went to answer it.

"Barbara thank you for coming on such short notice," He stepped out of the way and motioned Barbara to enter. She walked in giving Richard a wary look. "Please come in." He gave her a small hug. "Would you like to have something to drink?"

"Tea if it's not too much of a bother." Barbara padded to the dining table and placed a lap top on top of it. She opened the top and turned it on, a faint whine emitted from it.

Miranda came in hugged Barbara and kissed her on the cheek. "It's so nice of you to help us. I'll get Addison." She left the room and knocked on Addison's door. "Addison, Barbara Jenkins is here.

A moment later the two came into the dining room. Addison walked slightly behind Miranda, as if to hide and stood behind a chair with her head down. Over the tops of her eyes, she peeked at Barbara. Barbara sat in a chair and glanced up at her. Her warm brown eyes didn't portray any malevolence and her smile seemed genuine. Addison relaxed, just a little.

Miranda put her hand on Barbara's shoulder, "Addison

this is Barbara Jenkins, Barbara this is Addison..." Miranda turned red. "Why we completely forgot to ask you your last name."

"Johnson," Addison said timidly.

Barbara's smile grew. She was aware that Addison was uncomfortable. "Addison, no matter what happens here tonight; be assured, I or CPS will not try to take you away. That being said, I can really get into a lot of trouble," she said looking from Miranda to Richard and then to Addison, "for not reporting this. So I hope you all will keep this under your hats." They each nodded. Addison relaxed her shoulders and sighed. "These are good people Addison. I wish there were more like them in our registry." Barbara scanned her screen and began typing. "First of all tell me about you. How old are you, what families you have been with, especially the last one." Addison related everything she could remember. Barbara's fingers ran across the keyboard as fast as a spider's leg scurries to get away from an enemy.

Addison watched Barbara's facial features as she typed and listened to the clicking of the keys. She watched as her eye brows furled and she pursed her lips. She noted the frustration in her face and then she'd start typing again.

Barbara asked Addison questions about the families she lived starting with the last. Addison tried to remember everything, but she was too young at the time to be accurate. Barbara's fingers produced an innumerable amount of clicks from the computer. She finally stopped and looked up at Addison. "Are you sure your name is Addison Johnson?"

"Yes," Addison said and nodded. She squinted at Barbara with ice blue eyes. The furrow of her brows showed her confusion or concern, or a combination. "Why do you ask?"

"Because," Barbara replied, "I can trace your history back to when you were ten, but before that nothing. Did you come from another state?" Addison shook her head slowly.

"Could there be a misspelling error of some kind?" Richard asked as he moved to peek over Barbara's shoulder.

"That can be a possibility." Barbara slowly nodded. "Let me see what I can come up with."

Barbara proceeded to type again. After twenty minutes, she blurted out, "There." She eyed Addison with a gleam of success. "Well it seems your name isn't Addison Johnson." Addison had a look of fright on her face. Barbara turned her lap top around so that Addison, Miranda and Richard could see the screen. "You're Madison Johansson. Somehow the spelling of your name was entered incorrectly." Madison/Addison gaped at Barbara. *This is why I could never find Izzy. If someone could have spent more time and do a thorough search.* She started to cry.

Miranda put her arm around Madison and held her. She turned to the screen and saw a photograph of a very young version of Madison and a girl who looked just like her now and a mother Madison would grow up to resemble. It didn't take a detective to realize that she was looking at a family, Madison's family. All three had straight black hair and the same ice blue eyes. Their smiles all dimpled at the same spots. Written in pen were the names Naomi, Madison and Elizabeth. They were all smiling in front of a statue in a park.

Richard got up and stepped closer to the screen. "Why, we know that park," he said in wonder and looked at Miranda.

She smiled, "That's our park. We used to spend summer afternoons there." Seconds flew by as she remembered one day long, long ago. "We had an apartment in that neighborhood. You were in Viet Nam. I wrote to you and told you I was pregnant with Elizabeth." Her eyes were glistening. *How could I have forgotten about that park? We lived for ten years until we found this place.*

Madison stared at the picture of her family. Her fingers moved to touch the image of her mother and sister, but she stopped not wanting to smudge Barbara's screen. Barbara nodded. Madison shook her head. She turned to both and asked, "Can you take me there sometime?"

"Yes, if the weather's good we can go tomorrow," said Richard. "I should like to find the bench I carved our initials on." He squeezed Miranda's arm. She put her hand up to his and returned the squeeze.

Madison beamed. Tears fell. She couldn't say anything, she felt too overwhelmed. She was gazing at her almost forgotten life. The one she longed to return to, although, she knew it wouldn't be the same, her mother was gone. At least she'd walk through the park where the picture was taken. Memories might come back. She sat back in her chair and thought of all the times she looked for her sister.

Moments later, "I've found your sister," Barbara blurted out, "at least her last address, it was from two years ago." She gazed at the three in triumph. "Do you have a pen and paper?" Miranda raced to Richard's desk to get the items and rushed back. Barbara wrote down the address and a telephone number and handed it to Madison.

She took the paper and held it as if it were going to bite her. Her hand shook as she stared at the numbers and letters through blurry eyes. After a minute her frozen expression thawed and turned into a wide beaming smile. Miranda kissed the top of her head.

Richard yanked a handkerchief from his pocket and blew his nose, "Damn cold."

Everybody turned to him and laughed. It was time for laughing and time for merriment.

"Thank you," Madison said to Barbara, "for helping me." She turned to Miranda and said, "Thank you for taking me in and helping me find my sister."

Looking at Richard, Barbara said, "Can I use your printer, I'll make a print of the photo for Madison." Five minutes later she closed her laptop and stood up. "I think, I helped out all I could for now. Madison, I think you should call your sister before you go see her. It will come as a big enough surprise just hearing you. The number and address may not be good, but it's the last known address we have for her. I hope you find what you are looking for." She turned to Miranda, "If there are any complications, you know where to find me. I'll help anyway I can."

"We'll take your advice," Miranda got up and hugged Barbara. "We owe you a night out on the town. I expect you to collect it," she said with a smile. "We'll make it a night to remember."

Richard shook her hand and escorted her out to the door. "Thank you." He gave her a small hug and a kiss on the cheek.

Barbara turned as she was about to exit, "I'll be in my office all day tomorrow, let me know what happens." She left happier than she felt in a long time.

After Richard closed the door and returned to the dining room. "I think that went well," he said smiling, hands clasped behind his back arching up and down on his feet, "don't you?"

Madison sat staring down at the image of her mother and sister, jumped up and bowled him over throwing a bear hug around him. He gently put his arm around her and stroked the back of her head.

CHAPTER NINE

THE NEXT DAY MADISON GOT UP EARLY, actually she never really slept. She just couldn't shut down her mind. Memories crept up and bubbled like hot soup in a pot on the fire. Despite being sleep deprived she was loaded with nervous energy and it made it hard for her to stand still for more than a minute. A clock on the mantle said it was five-thirty A.M. She plumped down onto the sofa, got up and moved to the window then to a chair. She tried to be as quiet as possible, not wanting to wake Miranda or Richard, but she couldn't relax and kept moving and with moving came sound. She changed her position ten times in five minutes and each time willing the clock to hurry. Exasperated, when she finally settled down the clock had just changed ten minutes.

She couldn't believe her luck. She hadn't known the Cramers more than a few days and already they helped her to do what she spent years trying to achieve. Of course, Barbara did all the work, but it was the Cramers who brought them together and Barbara accomplished it in a snap of a finger.

Taking the photo, Madison looked at it for the hundredth time. She stared at the teen-age girl who looked to be about twelve and her mother who appeared to be young, maybe early thirties. She tried to memorize every feature on that piece of paper. Every feature burned slowly in her mind. Once there, always ready to be brought up at a second's notice. Her smile widened and widened until the ends of her mouth were in line with the bottoms of her ears, at least it seemed so. Tears came whenever she thought of her mother, the image lost to a child's memory, but now her image stared back at her from the paper she held. Her mother's eyes seemed sad in some way; they seemed to say, "Remember me." Was this the last picture of the three of them together? A tear dropped on the edge of the paper and Madison quickly dabbed it away. She didn't want anything to ruin her only photo of her family.

Madison didn't know when the picture was taken, but it had to be at least ten years ago, for she looked three or four tops. She was amazed at how the three of them looked so much alike, as if we were stamped from the same mold.

She looked up at the clock, both hands stood in a straight line with the long one pointing to the six. The second hand ticked slowly to the right and seemed to slow as it rose to the nine position. Madison heard a door knob turn, then shuffling feet. Richard came around the corner.

"Did you get any sleep?" He asked. Madison shook her head slowly. "I didn't think you would. Do you want a cup of coffee?"

"Yes please." She got up and followed him into the kitchen. "Can I help you?"

"Look its Sunday. We'll call at ten. Some people sleep late." He saw her disappointment. "O.K. we'll call at nine."

He tweaked her nose. "But no earlier." Madison smiled.

Madison sat on the sofa wringing her hands, the seconds wouldn't speed fast enough to turn into minutes and the minutes slugged refusing to turn into hours. During this wait she concentrated on the photograph. She smiled occasionally until her gaze returned to the clock.

Minutes later Miranda came out and smelled the aroma of freshly brewed coffee. "Um, that smells delicious. Is there any left for me?"

Richard nodded and went to fetch his wife a cup. Meanwhile Miranda gazed at Madison. She knew how Madison felt, waiting for something as important as this. It brought her mind back to the day Richard was transported to Hawaii from Viet Nam. Miranda was a nurse at one of the hospitals. She had heard Richard had been wounded in a battle. The Navy flew him and sixty other wounded Marines to a naval hospital. She remembered watching as the plane grew from a speck in the sky to landing on the tarmac. It seemed to take hours.

Miranda closed her bathrobe tightly around her and sat next to Madison. She put her arm around her and squeezed. Madison glanced at her then back to the clock, willing it to move faster. Miranda kissed the side of Madison's head.

"Waiting has never been one of my strong suits." Miranda said.

Richard gave Miranda a cup and she sipped it slowly, "Ooh, that is good," she said looking up at him. "You should make it more often."

With a twinkle in his eye Richard replied, "I'll have you know, I was the best coffee maker in the three of four.

WHOORA."

Miranda leaned over to Madison and whispered, "That's a Marine term. Just pretend you know what he said and smile."

Miranda and Richard tried to take Madison's mind off the time. They asked her a thousand questions. Each of which didn't seem to have any relevance to the situation at hand. Madison, perturbed, was about to make that point when she realized what her two friends were doing. She sat back and looked at the clock and smiled.

"Thank you."

Both gawked at her perplexed and then at each other and smiled.

"See," said Richard, "I told you she's sharp." He looked at the clock and then his watch. "Go ahead," he said to Madison, "Its eight o'clock go ahead and make the call." He handed her his cell phone.

Madison extended her hand hesitantly. She licked her lips and scratched her head staring at the small device in her hand. Her finger moved to the buttons but stopped before they could make contact.

"Well?"

Miranda held out her hand for the phone.

"Would you like me to call for you?" Miranda asked.

"Please." Madison said and handed over the phone.

Miranda punched in the numbers from the paper on the table. She let the phone ring twice and smiled at Madison.

Madison scraped her hands on the legs of her pajamas. She was bouncing slightly on the couch trying to expend pent up energy. She heard, 'Hello.' The voice sounded cautious. In the back ground she could hear, 'Mommy who is it?' Tears streamed down Madison's face.

"Good morning," said Miranda cheerfully, "Is this Elizabeth Johannson?" Richard scooted to the edge of his chair.

"Uh, yes." The voice said hesitantly, "Who are you?"

'Mommy who is it?' Madison could hear a little girl's voice and she imagined her trying to grip her mother's arm. "Shush Tilley mommy's trying to find out who it is."

"Elizabeth, did you have a sister named Madison?" Silence. It stretched for some seconds. "Hello?"

"I'm still here." The voice was flat. The separation of the two sentences took years. "Why do you ask?"

"Madison would like to talk to you." Miranda looked at Madison and nodded smiling.

"Look," the voice turned to anger, "if this is a joke, it's cruel and I don't find it the least bit funny."

"Elizabeth, I assure you this is not a joke." Miranda hurried to say, expecting Elizabeth to hang up. "Let me put Madison on the phone." She handed the phone over.

"IZZY," Madison blurted, "It's me Madison." She heard, 'Oh God,' and the sound of the phone dropping and a little girl asked what was wrong. "Izzy, Izzy are you still there?" This time the noise was of someone picking a phone off the floor.

"Maddie?" Elizabeth asked, her voice trembling with a hint of uncertainty.

"Yes Izzy it's me." She cried into the phone. "God, I'm so glad we found you. I tried so hard, but it seems that CPS had my name spelled wrong and all I remembered was that your name was Izzy. I thought was short for Isadore and Isabel. Izzy, I tried so hard to find you."

"Maddie where are you?" This voice sounded different, as if it was filled with wonder and excitement.

'Mommy, mommy who is Maddie?" The little voice kept asking. There seemed to be fright in that little voice.

"Tilley it's your Auntie." The little voice said, 'My Auntie.'

Madison heard the words 'Auntie' but it didn't register. *Wait! I'm an aunt. Not only did I find my sister, but she has a child.*

"Maddie where are you? Are you in the city?" Elizabeth asked. Excitement grew by the second.

"Yes, we're in Manhattan, where are you?" Madison cried into the phone. She forgot she had an old address. Tears streamed from her eyes.

"Me too. We live down near Battery. Can we meet today? I can come to you or you can come here." The words couldn't come out fast enough. Elizabeth didn't want to take the chance that there would be a lost connection before plans could be made. "Where do you live?"

Miranda took the phone from Madison, "Elizabeth this is Miranda Cramer and Madison is living with us," she looked at her ward. Madison sat tensed. "If you like we can have lunch here at our place, say noon?"

"Yes, yes I can be there." Elizabeth said quickly. "I have a little girl, can I bring her with me?" Her voice was hesitant.

"Of course you can," said Miranda. "We would love to meet the both of you." She gave her the address and the phone back to Madison.

Madison and Elizabeth talked for a few minutes and then she pressed the disconnect button.

Miranda and Richard sat on the edges of their seats; both eyed Madison with mouths open waiting for her to say something. Madison stared into the past with a small smile on her face. She held the phone in her hand staring at the black screen. A dark image of her gazed out at her, but it didn't reflect how she felt. The phone's image didn't portray a young woman who just had the only family she had handed to her. She looked at the smiling image and bolted up.

"I'm an aunt," she blurted out. "I'm an aunt," only this time, her voice was filled with wonder. "An aunt, Aunt Madison, Auntie Maddie." She tried each variation several times, testing to see which one fit better. "Yes! Maddie. Now I remember Izzy used to call me Maddie." She smiled as she twirled around and fell onto the sofa. *Madison sounded so formal, like someone you would announce if they were entering a ball or any other formal affair.* She looked at the couple and whispered, "I'm an aunt." Her eyes lit up and a smile grew, "I'm an aunt."

Richard clapped his hands and stated, "I think that we should prepare for company."

"What do you mean by that Richard," Miranda said suspiciously, "Are you inferring that we need to clean. This place is spotless."

"No, no my dear, we need to go to the grocers." He said quickly. "We should have some treats for the little girl," and with a little more restrain, "and maybe for us. Maybe

something sweet." He gave Miranda a conspiratorial wink.
"Well, this is a special occasion," she said with a smile.

◆ ◆ ◆

Almost three hours later Madison bursting with excitement announced that she would wait for Elizabeth in the lobby. Richard went down with her. He said it would suppress any problems with the neighbors.

On the way down, Richard remembered, that just two days ago their trip in the elevator was quite different. Now, Madison acted lively and full of enthusiasm, whereas that night she stood stone still and frightened. Madison kept bouncing willing the elevator to descend faster.

"Madison," Richard said in a concerned voice, trying hard to keep from smiling, "bouncing up and down will not make the elevator go faster. It just gives us a bumpier ride."

She stopped and looked at him. After a few seconds the bouncing started again. He gave an exasperated moan and kept silent.

The elevator stopped and Madison took a step forward repeating, "Open, open, open."

A bell dinged and the door slid slowly. Madison was through before it fully open. She rushed to the glass windows and looked outside. People rushed left and right, all with their heads buried in their coat collars. No one took notice of the girl in the window standing on her tippy toes scanning the people coming from the left. The bouncing continued.

After a minute, "Do you think she got lost?" She asked Richard. He stood silently by her side.

"Madison it may take them a while to get here. She might have had trouble getting the right train or maybe getting your niece ready slowed her down." He laid his hand on her shoulder. "Don't worry, she'll come and we'll wait for her. Right here in the warmth of the lobby." He continued to scan the street for a woman with black hair.

The lobby was sterile. A glass-enclosed wall over-looking the street on one side with a bank of mail boxes on the opposite and the bank of elevators on the third. It contained only two paintings, replicas, on the opposite wall from the elevators with a setee in between them. Richard didn't spend time in the lobby and never paid attention to the art work. Now that he stood in one spot for more than a minute he was able to study them. He made a note to have them changed. Richard found quaint cottages nestled in an idyllic wood were not his cup of tea.

Madison had stopped bouncing, but now she shifted from one foot to the other at an alarming rate. Her hands twisted in each other as she had her head up to the window. Her breath showed in a cloud of moisture in an ever increasing circle. Suddenly she stopped and turned to look at Richard.

"Maybe I should go stand outside," she said. Her face portrayed a model of anxiety.

"All you'll do is get cold," he said with a smile. "But if it is your wish, I'll stand outside with you." Madison nodded. Richard opened the door for her and they stepped out into the freezing cold of New York City. They stood on the top step of the entry and scanned the street.

After about five minutes Madison began to feel the icy

chill of the near winter weather. She turned around and looked at the warmth of the inside of the lobby. Her breath formed a white cloud and her knees began to shake. She decided that Richard was right after all, it was foolish to wait out here when there was a perfectly warm lobby to wait in.

"Maybe you're right Richard." She said with red cheeks of embarrassment, or maybe it was the cold. "We should wait inside." Richard smiled and dug into his pocket for his pass key. Madison turned once more to look down the street.

In the distance, she spied a head bouncing up and down with perfect cadence. Even though the person was wearing a hat, Madison could see shiny black hair sticking out of the sides. People were walking in front of the woman but as they approached they moved out of the way. Madison's heart began to pound.

Richard started to open the door when he saw her expression and looked down the street. He too saw the woman and a smile grew as he watched Madison start bouncing again. She looked like a runner getting ready to jump out of the gate.

❖ ❖ ❖

Elizabeth couldn't believe her ears when she got the call this morning. She wanted to rush to her sister right then and there, but decided to get Tilley ready and to spruce up herself. Two hours wasn't a long time to wait when you've been waiting for ten years for something.

Tilley kept asking about her auntie. Why hadn't she met her before? Were they mad at each other? Did she not want to know me?

Elizabeth explained everything to her in a chronological order of the events as they took place. She told Tilley that after they were separated, they didn't see each again.

Did you miss her mommy? Will you be happy to see her again? Will she like me? I have an auntie now, don't I?

Elizabeth answered yes to all those questions and told Tilley they will be going to see her in a few minutes.

They too had to wait first for the train to upper Manhattan. Then the cross island train to the East side. It was hard for her to wait. She dreamt of this reunion a thousand times and gave up all hope of ever finding her little sister, but now she would see her in a matter of minutes.

They got off the subway and climbed the stairs. It took a while, Tilley's legs were short and she wanted to climb them by herself, because she was a big girl and now had an auntie. Once on the street Elizabeth set a fast pace. They were only two blocks from the address that was given to her.

Tilley found it hard to keep up with her mother and protested.

They were so close that Elizabeth decided to pick her up and carry Tilley to the address where her sister would be waiting.

❖ ❖ ❖

Madison wasn't sure that the woman who she saw was her sister. After all there must be thousands of women with black hair; she had approached many of them since living on the street. But when she saw her lean over and pick up a little girl with black hair, she knew.

"There she is," Madison screamed. She yelled so loud that passersby stared at her. She flew down the steps and up the street pushing aside anyone who got in the way. She charged, as the woman was crossing the street, screaming "Izzy," over and over.

Elizabeth put Tilley down as soon as they stepped up onto the side walk. She heard her name and looked up at Madison through the hustling pedestrians barreling toward them like some demented running-back hurling for the goal line. She grabbed Tilley's hand and bounded up the street to meet her sister. In the last few feet she let go of Tilley and crashed into her sister.

◆ ◆ ◆

Richard stepped out to the edge of the stoop and looked upon the scene from three steps up. He had a good view. He could see the joyous look on Elizabeth's face and the perplexed expression of the little girl she had just put down. Deciding to let them have their moment of undisturbed reunion, he watched them collide and twirl like ballerinas. People all around them hurried to get out of the way, afraid they might be caught by Madison's flying feet.

He felt happy for Madison, *she deserves this.* He watched as they hugged, uncaring about the furious stares and unhappy faces of people who had to move to one side or the other. They just looked into each other's eyes talking as fast as they could trying to get ten years of life into one moment.

Richard felt a hand on his arm and a soft kiss on his cheek. He turned, Miranda stood beside him smiling. He put his arm around her and gave a small hug.

"You're a good man Richard," she said with all the love she felt for him in the past forty years.

Richard stood still gazing into the eyes of the only woman he had ever loved. He hadn't felt this good since he retired. He stroked Miranda's cheek with bare fingers.

"I had the help of a good woman."

ACKNOWLEDGEMENTS

It takes more than one person to write a book, no matter how long it is.

I would like to thank Kit Crumb for his advice and story editing, Chris Molé for the cover, and my fellow writers at the Mission Coffee Writers Group (Fremont, California) who spurred me on and helped me refine what skills I do have.

ABOUT THE AUTHOR

FRANK MARSEGLIA was born in Bridgeport, Connecticut and enlisted in the Marine Corps in 1970. He met his wife, Sharon, in 1979 and they moved to Redwood City, California in the San Francisco Bay Area. Frank, Sharon, and their two children moved to Union City, California in 1987 and lived there for thirty years. After retiring in 2014, Frank started to write. He enjoys the process and loves to move between fantasy, horror and creative non-fiction. He and his wife moved to Ashland, Oregon in 2017.